PEREGRINE DREAM

Also by Ray Ring

Telluride Smile

PEREGRINE DREAM

RAY RING

ST. MARTIN'S PRESS
NEW YORK

Design by Jaye Zimet.

Library of Congress Cataloging-in-Publication Data

Ring, Raymond H.
    Peregrine dream / Ray Ring.
        p.   cm.
    ISBN 0-312-03909-3
    I.   Title.
PS3568.I567P47   1990
813'.54—dc20   89-24095
                                                               CIP

First edition
10 9 8 7 6 5 4 3 2 1

For Linda Ellen, my peach

My thanks to the wildlife researchers and other experts who provided background for *Peregrine Dream*, especially Bill Girden the falconer; Stephen Hale, Jim Jarchow, and Stephen Russell (all associated in one way or another with the University of Arizona); Kim Milenski; and Tice Suplee, Bruce Palmer, and Dave West of the Arizona Department of Game and Fish. Any inaccuracies herein, intentional or unintentional, are mine alone.

PEREGRINE DREAM

1

I'd been more or less awake for an hour, watching the darkness give way to the dawn, letting myself imagine that the process had some great significance. It was just as well I got interrupted. A pickup with one good headlight came crawling along the dirt road below my hiding place, banging over the washboards and muttering up the little hills, and stopped where the cattle gate blocked its progress. The headlight went off and the driver slid out; in the dimness, a whippy bearded man in a shiny leather jacket and a duckbill cap, shotgun in one hand and bolt cutters in the other. He didn't seem the least bit concerned about anything that might go wrong. I was one of those things. I was huddled on the stony overlook where I'd lasted the night in a cold camp, no fire, no coffee, no whiskey. Well, without two of the three, anyway. I had a clear view of him ambling toward the gate, but I didn't concentrate on it; people can sense when they're being watched. I looked beyond him, out over the desert that seemed soft and inviting. Once the sun was up, that would change. He grunted as he forced the cutters through the padlocked chain that secured the gate, the loose ends of the chain clinking down, and he kicked the gate open. That made him officially my business.

He drove on in. The road wasn't much of a road, just two wheel ruts winding along the flank of a ridge, and he had to take it slow. I trailed after him on foot, keeping to the higher ground and cutting the inside curves, dodging cactus and mesquite and shindaggers, jogging when I had to. It was fine for ten minutes and less fine after that, but before too long we ran out of room. The road ended against the Santa Catalina range, in under the rock cliffs.

Three hundred feet straight up, sunlight was just touching the top of the rock and making it glow red. Down below we were still in the shadow of mountains off to the east. It was one of those spectacular moments that come anytime in the West, when you least expect them and even when you do. The band of sunlight steadily intensified, creeping down the rock, emphasizing its immensity and belittling us.

He drove as far as he could and got out and trained binoculars on the rock, while I caught my breath and used my own binoculars to learn more about him.

His pickup was a beige short-bed Chevy, recent, dented and scratched by thorns and looking twice its age. The license plate had been smeared with mud. The bed held a jumble of gear I couldn't identify. Wedged against the cab were two boxes, unpainted plywood, windows screened by chicken wire. I couldn't make out what was in them. I couldn't tell much more about him either, except that he was willing to appear in broad daylight in a duckbill cap. After a while he had his binoculars aimed at the sky. He was watching a bird.

I glassed it, and there was no mistaking that silhouette, the long raked wings and streamlined tail, the way it cut the air. Goddamn him. He was after a peregrine.

He set his first trap in a sandy wash. The nets had a fine open weave that made them just about invisible, and he strung them belt high, one behind the other about six feet apart, on angle irons that he pounded into the sand. The bait was an uncooperative pigeon that he pulled from one of the plywood boxes in the pickup. He palmed the pigeon, tied its legs on a short leash to a pipe wrench that he plunked down between the nets. The pigeon flapped wildly against the wrench and got nowhere. Duckbill stepped back and fired up a deadly cigar stub and studied his setup, lowered one of the nets a few inches, nodded.

Over the next hour he baited another trap a quarter mile away and then surprised me by flinging out more pigeons here and there along the road, tied to odds and ends from his toolbox, so they flopped around right where they landed. There was something strange, and I glassed them. These pigeons had been laced into little black vests, like sexual fetishes, and there were tiny nooses dangling all over the vests, so anything coming in for a grab would get itself snared.

The peregrine had gone away. The man in the duckbill cap, the pigeons, me, we were all watching the sky. Waiting. He had stashed the pickup in a thicket and climbed into a jumble of boulders and I'd tucked myself in a crease just above him. Now and again I got an acrid whiff of his cigar. It got warmer and he took off his jacket, revealing a T-shirt that had the slogan about how I could make his day. The sun was about to touch us. The cliffs looming over us glowed like a gigantic hot coal.

In unison the pigeons struggling around the landscape grew more frantic, and then all of them hunched against the ground. I spotted it again: the peregrine, soaring in tight circles far overhead, selecting a target. It went into a steep climb, hammering its wings the way they do, topped out, fluttered for an instant, folded and dived. Nothing could move that fast—it streaked at the nearest pigeon, ripped a net off the frame, surged skyward in a tangle and dropped onto the sand. The peregrine was down.

He got over there with the truck, jumped out and cautiously approached his catch. The peregrine was all fouled up, attacking the net in furious bursts. He kneeled on the net, murmuring apologies, chewing on that cigar. He had put on thick leather gloves that protected him to his elbows. He seemed to sense that what he was doing was innately sad.

2

The peregrine hissed at him. It tore at his gloves with talons and a sharply hooked beak below the fiercest stare. He had to eclipse that stare. He worked in close and laced a leather hood down over it, and as if a switch had been turned off, the peregrine stopped fighting.

He untangled the net and slipped it out, holding its wings against its body, trying not to break feathers. It was no larger than a crow but far more dangerously built, with the brawny shoulders, and more handsome, slate blue on the wings and back and an ivory breast descending into a pattern of fine brown dashes, legs bright orange, talons a wicked black. Even blinded by the hood, it was a prince of a bird. He had a straitjacket ready for it, made of a nylon stocking with the toe cut out.

He shoved the peregrine into the nylon until its head poked out the hole and snapped thick rubber bands around the package, sucking smoke out of his cigar butt. The peregrine panted. It clawed at the nylon. He tipped it over in the sand and bound its legs and talons with masking tape. The peregrine could do nothing then.

I would have gone down there and dealt with him. I would have done something for that peregrine. But that wasn't my job. I was being paid to watch, and I found out just how badly

I needed the money while he rerigged the trap, took his catch into the cab of the pickup, and drove back into cover.

Another hour dragged by, until there was a streak at the far set of nets, a *whap* and another peregrine brought down. The second one was the female, slightly larger and angrier than the male. He got it hooded and bound in another nylon, snapped on the rubber bands, finished with the tape job, all the time puffing on that ugly cigar stub, or another one just like it. For all I knew he bought them that way by the case. He had to squint a little when the smoke got in his eyes, but that was the only trouble he had.

He laid the female on the seat next to the male, and got busy loading all his gear: the nets, the pigeons, and the rest of it. Then he flipped what was left of the cigar into the sand and drove out, away from the cliffs. I huffed to stay with him, "Come on, come on," but he built a lead until I got to where I'd hidden my old four-wheel-drive Scout. It took me bouncing up and over and down to the road behind him with some of my teeth intact. I chewed his dust for the eight miles out to the paved highway, hanging way back so he couldn't see he was being tailed. He swung west toward Tucson, and so did I. The radio said it was already a hundred and one, hot even for June. The closest thing I had to air-conditioning was whatever they put on: Tammy Wynette, and then an old Patsy Cline. I wanted him to be keeping those falcons cool. I wanted him, period.

He turned off before Tucson, onto another dirt road that wasted itself through a loose neighborhood of trailers and clapboard houses that hadn't been much to begin with, and that was some time ago. The place he pulled into was four or five acres fenced by oxidizing chain link: cactus, sheds, piles of bald and torn tires, a truck frame up on blocks and the body parts strewn around, an empty corral and one of those ribbed sheet-metal Quonset huts that the military unloaded on an unsuspecting civilian population. He stopped at the hut and got out, carrying a paper grocery sack that could have held two falcons to go, and strolled inside. Forty-five minutes went by, one by one. I was parked down the road a lifetime from any shade. The radio said it was ten o'clock and a hundred and two. I was running out of sweat.

There was an unpainted sheet-metal mailbox cocked on a creosote-stained post where his driveway began. I noted the address and looked inside: a catalogue and a bill from a feed store, addressed to Artie Jackson. I could take him or follow instructions. I decided on business before pleasure, because I couldn't afford not to.

3

Edwina Garrett hiked along the row of cages under the tall cottonwoods behind her house, peering in at what she had: a batch of yelping coyote pups, a three-legged raccoon, a great horned owl favoring a bandaged wing. She pinched a nugget of something out of her pocket and flipped it through the bars to a one-eyed badger that was padding back and forth, back and forth. The badger ignored her.

She stared at it and asked me, "You're certain the birds he took were peregrines?"

"I'd say so."

"You know there aren't supposed to be any left around here." She made it a question.

"I know what I saw," I told her. "Before I quit Game and Fish, I was in on the first statewide count. We didn't locate many of them, but enough to remember what they looked like."

"You're a man of surprising talents."

I was past forty, slowing down and losing hair. I wore clothes. I had a beard that came and went. Right then it was coming. "I vary," I said.

She looked at me and scowled. It was very convincing.

She had never been a handsome woman, and she refused to make allowances. Her face was too long and severe, imperious brown eyes embedded close together under an overhanging brow, too much nose and lips, hair of Navajo wool, gray and sparse and tousled. Her shoulders stooped, making her appear thick in the body. Her hands were too large and her fingers too long, and her dress too much brown corduroy with too many pockets. Below were her varicosed calves and thick ankles swelling out of her walking shoes, dull brown leather with new white laces. On her those laces were racy.

She was not adorned by makeup or jewelry, and there were hairs growing out of her where nobody wanted to see them. Her skin was an indictment against seventy-one years in the desert. I hoped I looked as good as she did when I got to be her age.

"And he captured both of them?" she asked. "A breeding pair?"

"Yes."

Her scowl deepened. "This is bad, very bad."

"I can take care of it."

She strummed her fingernails across the bars and the badger stopped his pacing and waddled closer. She reached in and scratched its nose. The badger blinked its eye.

"You knew the falcons were up here, didn't you?" I asked.

After a moment she answered, "I can tell you exactly where on that cliff they're nesting, and how many young they have, and what day they were born, and when they'll fledge."

"You must have suspected he was going after them."

"Some yahoo has been breaking through that old cattle gate every time I turn around. I hired you to check it out. I didn't know it was this Artie Jackson scouting my falcons."

"Your falcons."

"They might as well be. They nest on my land. I provide them with a sanctuary."

"I could've stopped him right there."

She drew herself up. "I make the decisions on my land. Nobody else. And I don't do it hastily. You've made your report, as rudely as possible. Now I decide. You want to quit me too?"

I let that go by. "It rankled me, watching him get away with it. If you need a better reason, it's even against the law: peregrines are on the endangered list."

"There's some disagreement over the listing."

"There is over every listing. But whether there are only fifty mating pairs in the country or three hundred and fifty, we can't afford to lose any more. He probably plans to sell them to some falconer. There's a black market, and the limited supply has driven up prices. They say no bird packs as many thrills."

"I believe you do care."

It was a tough thing to be accused of.

"You are a surprising man," she said again.

She hiked over to a lidless plastic cooler propped beside one of the cottonwood trunks, where she had bottles on ice. The bottles were Mexican beers. Not Coronas. She gazed at them without fondness. "Will you have a beer, then?"

"And then what, some tennis?"

"Just let me think a little bit."

She lifted a couple of beers and levered off the caps with an old-fashioned wooden-handled opener. She thrust a bottle at me and asked, "Who said we were going to let him get away with it?"

4

She sat us down at a picnic table made of gapped pine slabs layered in varnish that had turned orange and cracked. The table abutted the crumbling stucco house and I could look in a grid of windows at a sagging couch in front of a monumental flagstone fireplace that was heaped with newspapers. Some of the windowpanes were broken but still holding together. Her whole place was like that. The giant cottonwoods gave us shade.

"I want you to understand about my land," she said. She gulped her beer and blotted her lips with the back of a shaky hand. None of that got into her voice. "Nineteen hundred and thirty-seven acres; that's one way to define what I have here. You've seen the cliffs. That's another way. And the falcons. That's what my land means. There's year-round water: springs popping up, and a creek that's reliable as any in Arizona. Grass, good native grass, grazed by deer, and bighorn sheep drifting down the mountain. I've got cactus all the way up to piñon pine, every acre wild, natural. And I'll go on keeping it that way as long as I can."

She paused again and glared, not at me so much as at the world. Sweat fled down her temples.

"I called it a sanctuary," she said. "Well, that's what it is. Nobody—and I mean nobody—has permission to hunt or fish or trap or dig up or cut down anything anywhere on my land. Nobody goes four-wheeling through it, nobody hikes it, nobody camps on it, and if I had my druthers, nobody would fly over it either. A dozen kinds of hummingbirds make their home here. Bobcats, ringtail, fox, quail, hawks, rattlers, Colorado River toads: you name it, I've got it right here. The whole Southwest used to be just like this, but there isn't much left. It's all been developed, overrun, fouled up one way or the other. I'm holding the line on my land."

As if in sympathy the coyote pups began to yip. "Simmer down," she yelled. "You eat better than I do." She waved off the cages and the animals in them. "I take in the casualties of all this progress. Got to have a license from the state of Arizona to do it; they consider it wildlife rehabilitation and put out a ream of regulations I try to ignore. I get the crippled, sick, and dying, the shell-shocked, the orphans. Golden eagles to kangaroo rats, tarantulas minus a couple of legs. People find 'em and bring 'em in, hit by trucks and cars, zapped by power lines, run ragged by dog packs, snared in traps, shot up by bored kids with twenty-twos or just starved because their range has been bladed over and covered in concrete, divided into lots, cut apart by roads. Nothing kills more efficiently than a road. Except maybe the chamber of commerce. I've got the evidence right here. The aftermath. Don't get me going."

She gulped beer and landed the bottle on the table. "It's no accident those peregrines found refuge up on my cliffs," she said. "Where else would they have a better chance of making it?"

"It wasn't enough of a chance."

"No." The word socked her. She had another swig of beer. "I get the cheapest they have, got an amigo brings it up from the interior, where you get full count on pesos to the dollar. I can't tell the difference anymore. My taster's shot." She stuck out her tongue and pointed at it.

I was supposed to laugh. I tried.

"You'd prefer whiskey," she said.

"I'd prefer that you explain the rest of the job."

"I was only trying to be sociable," she snapped. "I don't get many visitors, even ones I'm paying for."

"Look," I said. "What you stand for is pretty well known around here. You're something of a celebrity, such as we have. I know about you and your old man; Tyler Garrett underpaid half the men in this county fifty years ago, when his copper mine was going full bore. I know how he left you this land and how you're trying to make up for what he did to the other side of the mountain, where he scoured out the river and put in that smelter and turned another good piece of ground like this into a tailings dump. I know that ever since he died you live the pure life out here all alone with the animals, and I don't care if you really want company or if you enjoy scaring people off."

"Boo!" she said. It amused her. She celebrated by sliding more of the beer past her taster. "You do get rankled. I didn't mean to imply you were bought and paid for."

"I am. Maybe not today or tomorrow, but in the long run, everybody is. I'm touchy about it."

"Now you sound like T.G." She stretched out a smile that had the opposite meaning. "That's what everybody called him. Even me. He didn't like the sound of Dad, thought Father was what you called holy men, which he was anything but. He was just T.G. For years it was only him and me in this house. My mother balked at coming west. She had the notion civilization didn't reach this far. We managed to prove her right."

She seemed to live on the edge of anger, ready to jump at the slightest provocation. Maybe T.G. could have explained it.

"Such a knowing person as yourself," she said, "should have no problem figuring out what I want. My falcons. Retrieve them from this bird-napper, before he puts them into slavery, or sells them off to somebody who'll be harder to locate. I want them back in the nest by tonight, so the young ones don't go hungry. And discourage him from coming on my land ever again."

"Discourage him."

"That's right. And do a thorough job of it. I get the feeling you'd do it anyway, whether I paid you or not."

"It'll be more professional now."

"I want it done discreetly. No law involved. They aren't as reliable as they used to be."

"Not since they got dropped off T.G.'s payroll."

"Don't act so shocked. You're the only one on the payroll now. T.G. pissed away what he had and left me barely enough to live on. So I don't have much pull with the ones running things today, not enough to keep this quiet if I took it to the sheriff. He'd make it news, and I've had some of that aimed at me before, stories about what I'm trying to save here, and after every one I had a rush of people you wouldn't believe, trying to bag a deer, joyriding up my washes, lighting bonfires and partying all night and leaving behind all their trash and broken beer bottles. You can imagine what would happen if it got around I have peregrines. They'd be sneaking in any way they could, just to get a glimpse. There's nobody more persistent than a bird-watcher."

That did make me laugh.

"Well, it's true," she said. "They'll go to any lengths to fill out a life list."

"Don't you watch birds?"

"Not the way they do. I don't have to get acquainted with every last one on earth."

"Now you surprise me."

She wiped the sweat off her cheeks with her hand and lipped the beer, coughed, thrust out her arm and emptied the bottle into the dirt, and finished by sliding her tongue between her lips, spitting daintily. "Bug in there, doing laps. Dyer, what I care about is protecting what's mine. Whether or not the Audubon Society comes swarming up here, the more people who hear about these peregrines, the more chance somebody else will decide to trap them, or shoot them as trophies. That's how Audubon got his start, you know. With a shotgun."

"I know."

"If he was still alive, I could hire him for this job. But you'll have to do. Now get going."

5

Busting up a bird-napping, that's what I'd come to. Or backed into. I had reasons to be where I was, nothing dramatic. I wasn't an alcoholic, I hadn't been shot and crippled in the knee, I hadn't killed any innocent people and been haunted by the memory, I wasn't the victim of guilt or corruption or a vicious car wreck or no-fault divorce or junk food. I had none of those luxuries. I had only the little things to blame, like the way everyone else acted and thought the world should be run.

"Blow it yourself," had been my father's advice about life. "Don't let anybody blow it for you. Blow it exactly how you want it blown." The philosophy of Wild Horse Charlie, who raised me out of a cowboy trailer he towed around the West behind a succession of pickups, each one seeming a little older and more broken-down than the last, all of them sided with a version of his sign: WILD HORSE CHARLIE: HORSES BROKEN AND TRADED AND SHOED, WELLS WITCHED, FRIDGE AND WINDMILL AND CONVERSATION REPAIR, YOU NAME IT. After my mother left for good he took us and his stories and whatever pile of used books we happened to be lugging around then north as far as the Bitterroot country in Montana, but mostly we hung south in Arizona. "This stinking godforsaken desert is exactly how the world should appear," he'd say. "This is what we get for all our crimes against the planet and one another, a sentence of cactus and sand and rock. It isn't beautiful, but it's logical." And he'd take me out into it, walking or riding borrowed horses for days when we had the chance, but mostly driving the back roads, parking at the ranches where he earned meals and gas money for keeping this or that going until the next time he could make it by. It was a rough and independent life that was my only inheritance. When a flash flood got him in Redfield Canyon he had nothing except the old trailer, held together by duct tape and insulated by the books stacked against the walls, and a pickup that wouldn't start without a jump, and his collection of tools, and me, but a hundred people came to his funeral out at Redfield, where we left his ashes and nobody much goes.

After that I was free to blow it on my own. I did what he'd done for a while, against dwindling opportunity, as the old ranches were cutting back or being cut up for development, or just modernizing, mechanizing, computerizing, and throwing out what got broken instead of fixing it. And it took me that long to figure out I wasn't Wild Horse Charlie. Still, I couldn't come indoors, so I tried a little big-game guiding, until the hunting began to seem so one-sided I was pulling for the lions and bears—which is what got me in trouble later on, once I'd put myself through the university in what they call wildlife management and got on with the Arizona Department of Game and Fish, imagining all it meant was a paying job out on the land.

One sunny afternoon Game and Fish sent me wading up a creek in the Blue Range with a team of men and women armed with electric stun nets. We were going after some of the last surviving native Arizona trout. We were supposed to net as many trout as we could—zap each specimen with a precise voltage, the prescribed method for inducing temporary paralysis—and then take measurement and weight for a population study done on some computer. It was cold work that made us technicians and inadvertent executioners: lowered gently back into their home water, some of the trout just went belly up and floated away. There is, as the department likes to say, a certain attrition rate.

When the first floater went by I put down my net and sat on the bank thinking I hadn't set out to electrocute trout. A permanent notation was made in my file. It was joined by others as it took me a while to realize how completely I wasn't and never would be a department man. Coming out of college, I had inertia to work off, and the department did give me some jobs that made a little more sense, like doing search and rescue on the foolish and going undercover against poachers. Even then there was always desk work and waiting around to do the simplest things, bosses and regulations that had to be followed or surreptitiously ignored, and the steady pressure to approve the official line, and larger than anything the basic truth that the job wasn't as much about policing humans as policing wildlife.

Even now, after all that's gone down, the most terrible screams I've ever heard came from a pronghorn antelope netted from a speeding helicopter by a gang of biologists, who were hauling it off to a distant range to spread its species according to some master plan. And the bloodiest shooting I've ever had to witness was the prolonged shotgunning, again from helicopter, of a pack of coyotes racing desperately across the flats below. It's a standard method of predator control— which is what they really mean by "wildlife management": control.

Mainly I didn't like representing anything. I lasted eight years inside a uniform and a badge, and that was long enough.

I let a bear do me in. He was a problem bear; that's the official term, and maybe that's why I related. He'd been raiding the new picnic grounds in the Santa Ritas. Twice I'd had to go out and help trap and trank-dart him so he could be deported off somewhere he might not be so much bother— once we trucked him thirty miles south into the Harshaws, the second time sixty miles north into the Galiuros. But he was stubborn, a trait that's not appreciated in bears. He kept finding his way back across the desert and finally got to be a

17

regular player at the golf course that had been put in down in the foothills. This was the ultimate offense. The order was given to terminate; bears have no attorneys, or it might have dragged on. I was sent out with a rifle to do it. He'd been treed just off the ninth green, surrounded by a little crowd of golfers and their carts, caddies and gapers and one tiny Pekingese that made so much racket I almost shot it instead. I backed the crowd up and got an angle on the bear and lined him up in my sights. He was an old male who should have known better, but I guess he just didn't give a damn anymore; once all that land had been his to roam and he wasn't willing to give it up. I studied him through the sights and put my rifle back in the case and put the case in the department truck and left. A week later, I heard they'd run him down with a pack of hounds and done the job. By then my resignation had been accepted.

In the years since, I'd sort of holed up out at my place by the Coyote Mountains—forty acres of low-growth desert and the shell of an old adobe ranch house that I hadn't won in any poker game, or gotten as a payoff, or been willed by any shaman grandfather who was half-Indian and one with the cactus. I had just saved out of my paycheck and, before I quit and wrecked my credit profile for good, located an ultimate fixer-upper that was too far out for commuting and not near any lush water holes or soon-to-be highway interchanges or elegant views. It had room for Wild Horse Charlie's tools and some books and his last hand-lettered sign, and for me to feel apart from most anything, and most months I could make the payment without giving up too much of myself.

I used what skills I had to get by, and learned new ones. Somebody came to me wanting to war privately against cattle rustlers. Then somebody else's well was poisoned and I was hired to investigate the who and why. A boy hunting deer down in the Huachucas got shot and killed by a stray bullet on opening day, and his father asked me to find the shooter. And so on, until I realized I'd become sort of a detective, an odd and rustic one specializing in cases, such as they were, that came my way and that would keep me outdoors.

Over the years I had backed into where I was, but I had nowhere else to go than this desert, and there was nothing else I could be this late in life than an investigator of things like this bird-napping. Just like that old problem bear, I wasn't going to give it up. My secret was a low overhead.

6

The Scout was my sweatbox going back to Artie Jackson's place. The radio said it was a hundred and four. I turned in at the cockeyed mailbox and rumbled to the end of the coarsely graveled driveway and stopped at the Quonset hut. He must have heard me, but he didn't come out. People in the country usually do. His pickup was still there and I peered in the cab and saw no peregrines. A nervous rattling came from the cooler on top of the hut. Otherwise the hut was silent. I knocked on the door, whistling to show this was easy. A hole had been kicked in the door down low and patched crudely with plywood. No one came to the door. The windows on each side were scummed over like a parakeet's mirrors. I knocked again, tried the knob, and went in. It was one large room with a bare cement floor and the ribbed sheet-metal walls curving down. There was a musty barn smell. Hanging on pegs along one wall: rawhide harnesses, chains and ropes and leashes, leg-hold traps sized for muskrat up to bear. Along the other wall: the plywood pigeon boxes, sacks of feed, pellets scattered on the floor. Tacked to the back wall: pelts of bobcat, raccoon, coyote, fox, taken out of season and looking ratty. And snarling out at me back there, the mounted head of a javelina boar, tusks intact but eye sockets empty, the lower jaw held on by windings of electrician's tape.

20

I had a feeling. I stopped whistling and slid my revolver out of the belt holster and held it down by my side. Two light bulbs dangling on their cords had been left on. A western ballad played softly out of a radio on a shelf. There was a door back there, closed. Little noises came from the pigeons, and from something else at the back. I went that way. There was a particleboard workbench parallel to the wall, and behind it, stacks of stiffening skins, some on stretching boards, and a canvas tarp covering most of a packing crate. Something fluttered underneath. I flipped back the tarp and looked through the chicken wire top at the peregrines.

Dyer the pro. Sure.

They were tethered on perches, the leather hoods laced over their eyes. If they could see the wire, the cage, they'd attack it until they beat themselves to death. The male arched his long wings against the wooden slats, opened his beak, and stuck out his tongue at me. The female was calmer.

"Got you." The front doorway was loaded with a man: Artie Jackson, with the shotgun and the T-shirt slogan about making his day. I straightened up to face him, the workbench between us.

"Let's hear it," Jackson said.

"I was admiring the falcons."

He closed in, holding the shotgun on me, moving furtively, like a weasel. He had the face of one, and greasy eyes. "What falcons? Those are just a couple of prairie hawks."

"I know what they are. I was out there this morning when you trapped them."

The shotgun looked to be a twelve-gauge, but they all do from the barrel end. I had my little .38 aimed at his gut through the side of the workbench.

"What is this?" he demanded. "You got a badge?"

"Put down the shotgun, Artie. I'm private." I told him enough. I wanted it to go smoothly.

"This is some case you got for yourself. So the old broad misses her birdies." He laughed.

I told him about my gun and he stopped laughing. "You're

bagged," I ragged him. "You rather have the deputies out here? You've been trapping out of season—hell, Artie, everything you do is probably out of season. They'd make you a hobby."

"Bagged, hell. I got the twelve-gauge." He mulled it over, edgy from the strain. "I don't need this hassle. Maybe we can deal. You want the birds? Pay my expenses, kick in a little more so I get something out of it. Say, five hundred in all."

It was no deal I wanted, but I did my own mulling and concluded I could explain that once he rested the shotgun. "Deal," I said. With my left hand I pulled out my wallet and extracted the cash, my retainer for the case, and laid the bills on the bench. I got my money's worth: he lowered the shotgun. A smile nested on his beard.

"Now aren't we the civilized boys," he said.

He gathered the bills too casually and tucked them in the back pocket of his jeans, then tapped the shotgun on the falcons' cage. "The box isn't included. I got other uses for it. Wouldn't fit in that junker Scout you're driving anyway. I got something in back you can put the birds in."

I watched him disappear through the back door with the five hundred, heard him moving things back there. I looked at the falcons. The male pulled in his wings and shuffled along the perch, worrying his tether. The female waited. I yelled, "I didn't want them in nylons."

Jackson didn't answer. When he came back I'd finesse the shotgun and hold him up for my money and talk about how he'd learned the falcons were nesting on Edwina Garrett's land. If there were any others involved I had to discourage them too.

Sure.

The music on the radio got louder the longer I waited. He was taking too long. I went back there, into a smaller room jammed with rows of loaded-down steel shelves, rabbits in cages, fan belts up on more pegs, a bed, a sink. There was another door in the side wall, gaping open to the sunlight. The music on the radio seemed very loud. I started for the open door and then I saw Jackson in the corner, sprawled on the concrete, his shirt bloody. I bent down on one knee beside him. His throat was cut deeply and bubbles were rising and popping as he tried to breathe. He stared at me. There was a bloody razor knife lying next to us, and the shotgun. An engine started outside. I laid Jackson down and pulled out my gun and went out the side door into the brightness, and somebody backed the pickup fast right for me. I jumped, got hit, and slammed against the hut. The sun went away to a pinpoint and then it was gone.

7

There are ways to be brought back to consciousness, and being licked by a goat is not the worst by any means. This particular goat was a black and white nanny with soft pink eyes and fetid breath and a raspy tongue. I pushed it away and erected myself and leaned against the sun-broiled hut. That was mistake number two, or three; I'd lost count. The nanny bit the leg of my pants trying to make a meal. I knew how she felt.

The pickup and whoever had been driving it were long gone. I found my gun in the dried grass and took it back inside. Artie Jackson was right where I'd left him. He was done bleeding, his eyes locked open, his day made. The razor knife that made it hadn't been disturbed. His shotgun was lying where he'd dropped it, a token of futility. But in the big room where the falcons had been caged, there was nothing but bare gray concrete floor. Mistake number four. Or nineteen.

I poked around trying not to be frenzied and didn't find falcons in any of the other boxes, or up on the shelves, or in the drawers of the workbench, or in the trash can. I began to hear the music the radio had been playing all along: country western, every song with the melancholy undertow.

I stood there and wished I had a cigarette. I hadn't had one in a long time. I wished I had whiskey. I wished.

24

Good-bye, Artie Jackson, whoever you were. That's how it happens, smoothly, quietly, with one sharp effortless swipe of the razor while the line forms in the next room with the music on.

So he'd had company when I'd arrived, or somebody had sneaked in, somebody who didn't like the drift of our conversation, or who had some old business to settle. Somebody with the gumption to slice him, ram the pickup over me, park, and come back for the falcons. Or maybe somebody else altogether had paid a visit while I'd been sunning out in the yard, and the falcons were just too easy to pass up. Maybe four or five busloads had come through. I didn't know.

The case had suddenly gotten complicated. Cases tend to do that. My ribs hurt, and my legs, and the back of my head, and I was dusty and dry. I filled a paper cup with water from the dead man's tap and drank deeply. It was warm. All the tap water in southern Arizona would be, until October. Next April it would start heating up again. Maybe I'd have this case solved by then.

To proceed I needed clues. The back room had been home for Jackson. On a plywood platform there was a slab of foam rubber big enough to sleep two, made up neatly with sheets and two pillows and a Hudson's Bay blanket. The sheets featured a floral pattern. A sheet metal closet contained his clothes, and some pants and shirts and tomboy dresses for a size-ten woman. Socks and underthings for both of them were jumbled in steel drawers in a rack that was pasted with auto-parts decals. Dirty dishes and a pair of coffee mugs were piled in a steel utility sink, the rim of one mug bearing traces of garish red lipstick. Beside the sink was a small refrigerator, rounded the way they used to make them, cooling three cans of beer, an open package of sliced ham, mustard, mayo, half a loaf of white bread, and a frog floating in a jar. I held up the jar and looked at the frog. He was pickled, but free of mustard and mayo and lipstick kisses.

Jackson had kept his papers in the auto-parts dresser: more bills from the feed store, cash register receipts and unpaid local parking tickets, sections of topo maps marked with strings of Xs that I guessed represented his trap lines. No address book or checkbook. Nothing that seemed very significant.

On the wall by the phone was a bulletin board, pinned with hunting and fishing schedules issued by the state, and rippings from the local sports section: a record mule deer taken, a big fish hauled in, some columnist sounding off against trappers, Jackson's rebuttals scrawled in the margins in red pen. There was also an article about a new development going in on the city's far northwest side, a retirement community called Desierto Lindo. Jackson had penned exclamation points around that one. Maybe he'd been planning for his golden years.

Wedged into the frame of the bulletin board were two color Polaroids: Jackson clowning out in the desert with two huge men who had their shirts off, and Jackson hugging from behind a woman who had her shirt on. The woman was Hispanic, dark-haired and saucy, nearly as tall as Jackson, with definition of muscle on her arms and legs. She was wearing shorts and lace-up boots and a khaki short-sleeved shirt. She looked good, and bad: the flowered bed sheets and the naughty lipstick. The strange men in the other photo just looked bad; brothers, maybe twins, bulking with the muscle that comes from obsessive lifting, looming over Jackson, their eyes concealed behind granny glasses that were smoked black. They had long sun-faded red hair combed straight back, their skin was rusty with pale freckles, and one of them had something wrong with his grin: the left side of his face was inanimate, a lacework of scars. He was lifting Jackson off the ground with one hand. That was the joke.

There was no explanation on the back of the photos. I pocketed them. It's against the law to remove evidence from a crime scene in Arizona. I never did unless it was necessary.

The other things in Jackson's hut were just the spare parts of his fringe existence: whole and broken traps, carburetors, wheel rims, low-tech camping gear, the munitions of male and female vanity in the cramped bathroom, stashes of shells for the shotgun, vials of musk and other scents to be dribbled on his traps, the rabbits for food and for sale, the pigeons for bait.

To save myself from second thoughts I went so far as to search the pigeon boxes, and then the rabbit cages, making no friends and dirtying myself in the process. It seemed to be a comment on the state of detecting today.

The worst of it was the body. I tried to keep my eyes off his neck and the look on his face. He had a wallet with a driver's license for Artimus Stonewall Jackson that made him thirty-four the previous month, eighteen dollars and change, a pocketknife. No ring of keys; they'd be with the pickup. And he had my five hundred, folded in his back pocket. I watched myself crouching there, rolling him for the cash. Something else to remember.

The money had other implications. He hadn't been murdered for profit, or at least not for this cash. Which might mean the murderer hadn't been after the falcons either, and somebody else had sneaked in and snatched them. But not necessarily.

I was the bright one, all right.

The spotted nanny goat nipped me as I went outside and skimmed through the dust-layered storage sheds and wheelless vehicles and the horseless corral, fretting about the time it took, expecting to find nothing more, and succeeding.

That was the sum total of what I got out of Artie Jackson. There wasn't anything to indicate where the falcons had gone to. But my luck had to change. I heard the radio inside the hut still singing, and to prove how unhurried I was, I trudged back inside and shut it off. The hush settled heavily on me. When I got to the door I was too late to spook the woman who was pulling in. She whipped around in a yellow VW sand buggy, just missing the goat, rapped the engine and shut down and got out. She had the red lipstick on.

8

I opened the door and told her, "Bad news."

She was wearing the outfit from the photo: shorts, boots, the khaki short-sleeve, and she'd added a knotted red neckerchief that was paler than her lips. Her hair was banded in a full horsetail behind her square, solid face. Her skin was brown like my old desk chair. She looked me over, said, "You got trouble with that Scout, you talk to Artie."

"I've got different trouble. And so has Artie."

She moved one hand to the canvas purse slung from her shoulder. "Where is he?"

"In back, on the floor."

"Beat up or dead?"

"Look for yourself."

"You first."

I turned and walked through the hut to where Artie lay. His blood was darkening like a thundercloud.

"*Dios mío*," she whispered. Then, louder, "Dump the pistol." She had hers out of the purse, a stubby .22 with more of the electrician's tape wound around the cracked grips. It was the kind of countrified zip gun that trappers use to finish off their immobilized prey, barrel against skull for the fare-thee-well shot. She shoved the barrel at me.

I told her, "I just went through this with Artie."

Her eyelids fluttered, she swayed, caught herself. "Artie was a loser," she said. "I'm not."

"Forget about guns. Whoever killed him left in the pickup. Think about it."

She did, then asked, "Where were you?"

I told her that and a little more.

"Let's see some ID," she said. She endured reading the cards. Her features were blunt, primitive, Indian more than Spanish under the glossy lipstick and a load of eyeliner. She had a surplus of eyelashes and eyebrows, black hairs matting her arms, and a shadowy mustache that didn't take away from anything. "You must be hard up, going after some birds."

"They were important enough to steal. Twice."

"We weren't stealing them. You can't steal what's wild."

"It's done all the time. In a lot of different ways."

"One of those." She snorted.

"Tell me things. About you, about Artie. But mostly about where the falcons are now."

"Why should I?"

"It's me or the deputies."

"It's not either." But she let the zip gun sag. A scheming detective, she could relate to. "We had a buyer," she said. "Twenty grand for the birds, delivered in good shape."

"Twenty grand?"

"This guy had it to spend."

"Who?"

She scratched her leg with the zip gun. This went on.

"Five hundred was all Artie wanted to return the birds," I said.

"You come on like a cop; you had him scared. I said he was a loser, didn't I?" But he had been a little more than that, to her. She stared at his body. "Artie was working with some partners. The Reeds. *Dos gringos locos.* Maybe they killed him. I think they got the birds now."

I took out the photo of the big men. "The Reeds?"

She nodded. "Artie and me been together three years," she said. "Artie and them, longer."

"Which Reeds?"

"You mean names? Who knows? Maybe they never had any like regular people. They call themselves Reed One and Reed Two."

"One and Two?"

"I didn't make it up. This one with the scars is Reed Two. It's the only way to tell them apart."

"Where can I find them?"

"You don't want to." She thumbed over her shoulder. "Out in the desert. They camp out, run their traps, don't stay anyplace too long. Come in when they feel like it or got stuff to sell."

"They did business with Artie, why would they kill him?"

"Why not? That's how they'd see it." She stalked over and sat on the bed and shoved the zip gun into her purse, rummaged in there for one of those mini–whiskey bottles, the kind they serve on long flights, twisted the seal and drank it down. Her breathing had gotten ragged. She was stocky but very firm, with her legs shaved smooth. "Don't you care who I am?" she asked. "Lupe. Lupe Jackson. We were married." She snorted again. "He got me a ring out of a gumball machine in the courthouse lobby. It cost a quarter and it was plastic with a duck's face. It broke a couple of months later. I still carry the pieces."

I sat beside her. "Thirty-five years on this fucking planet, and that's about all I got," she said. "This deal was going to change that."

"Now it'll change things for the Reeds. Think they're going for the twenty thousand?"

"If they can pull it off."

I tried again. "Who's the buyer?"

She shook her head.

"Whoever it is," I said, "he could have bumped Artie without any help from the Reeds—like eliminating the middleman—and picked up the falcons for free."

She shook her head again. "That's for me to know. What do you care who killed Artie?"

"I care about falcons. Sooner or later, they'll wind up where the twenty grand is now. Everything flows toward money. You help me find them, there might be a payoff."

She didn't ask how much. She was considering other, more attractive options. Whatever thin rapport we'd had was gone, replaced by her own rapidly multiplying schemes. "Why don't you just get the hell out of here?" she said. "Go look somewhere else for your falcons."

"They aren't mine. They don't belong to anyone except themselves." I dumped out her purse, "Hey," she said, but she didn't come at me. She had fibbed a little. She had a hundred and forty-three bucks and no pieces of the plastic duck wedding ring. Her driver's license made her thirty-seven.

"Artie was no good with money," she said ruefully. "I handled it." She snatched the bills, the license, went for the zip gun a little too eagerly. I grabbed her wrist and twisted her around by it, up behind her shoulders, and hugged her around her neck. I snarled in her ear, "Take another look at Artie. This is beyond business now. This is murder, and it makes me awfully worried about those falcons."

"So?" she said.

She had a point. The dead man in the corner needed a cleanup crew and a number and a tucking-in by law and order. I couldn't be slowed by all that, but I could use it to keep things rolling.

I let her go and dialed 911 on the wall phone. A dispatcher answered after three rings and listened to me tell about the body and its address. I hung up without identifying myself and ripped the phone off the wall.

"Wow," Lupe Jackson said.

"You've got ten minutes before the deputies get here." I dropped her zip gun and walked out without looking back, got the Scout going down the driveway and onto the dirt road, driving fast and sending up a lot of dust. When I was out of sight I swung off into open desert, slammed into four-wheel, doubled back and up a little hill, and stopped when I had a good view of whatever Lupe Jackson was going to do next.

9

She went right for the money. It had to be that. She scurried
out to the corral and stabbed the ground with a bayonet, dug
up a glass jar about the size peanut butter comes in, and then
another one. Through the binoculars I could see wrinkled
green inside the jars. It didn't seem like twenty grand, and I
was sensitive to such things.

She took the jars and disappeared into the hut, came out
two minutes later lugging her purse and a backpack, pitched
them into the sand buggy and roared out. She led me to the
paved highway, and south down the french-fry strip into
the congestion of Tucson, attacking the traffic and heading
straight for the twenty-story thicket downtown. In its shad-
ows she circled for a parking space, found one and attacked it
too. I pulled in by a red curb and waited to see what would get
it next.

She slammed out, shouldered her purse, snubbed the
parking meter, and charged off with her horsetail hairdo
bobbing. I hiked after her, south two more blocks into the
historical district, where the street was walled with hundred-
year-old fortresslike adobes that had been renovated and
whitewashed and taken over by lawyers and architects and the
other Anglo gentry. The former occupants, Hispanics whose
ancestors had dug the mud and made the houses long ago, had

been pushed farther south, where the gas stations and drug dealers accepted food stamps, and any arguments about it would be out of range of downtown.

Lupe Jackson charged into one of the adobes, which was decorated by a familiar logo of a sun setting over mountain and stream: the Nature League. I got to the door, new and mostly glass, and looked in at an uncluttered office done in earth tones, where she was ranting at a sandy-haired man I knew, who was standing there looking stricken.

Disregarding his expression he was a dandy, trimly fit in a crepe emerald-green shirt, a cloth belt that matched, jeans that had been washed more than they'd been worn into pale blue sterility, and rubber-soled moccasins. Under his lanky well-maintained hair, parted on the side and swept back, his face had the handsome rugged look, but it hadn't been tested. His nose was thin and had never been broken, and he carried his chin forward, where no one who'd ever been socked would.

Lupe Jackson was about to fix him. I couldn't make out what she was saying, but she was angry and her gestures slashed at him. Then she pulled the little zip gun.

The shot was a pop, not anything to be noticed. He shouted and whirled and crashed to the floor, and I was going in. She snapped off a shot at me that broke the glass in the door and she scrambled away, deeper into the building. I had the .38 out, but there was nothing to shoot. The victim of the moment was leaving bloodstains on the slate gray wall-to-wall carpeting. He sat up with my help, gripping his left arm above the elbow. That's where the bullet hole was. The wound had calmed him. He looked at me with pale blue eyes that matched his jeans. His leaking blood matched his moccasins. He was that coordinated.

"Dyer," he said. "She shot me."

I told him to stay put and went after Lupe Jackson, through and out back to the courtyard, where she'd gone over the wall, tearing a swath in the ivy. On the other side was an alley. I started to boost myself over and heard him coming from behind.

"She's gone," he said. "She can outrun either one of us."

"You afraid I'll catch her?"

That seemed to shake him up more than being shot. Or it could've been the delayed shock. He winced and grabbed his bleeding arm and plopped down in a mesh iron chair that had been recently painted a peaceful white.

"Dyer the detective," he said.

I gave up on Lupe Jackson for the time being. He was probably right about her sprint versus mine, and anyway, I had him in the hand. Him, of all people.

"Why'd she shoot you, Cady?"

"You're asking me? I thought you put her up to it."

"Not with that little twenty-two. I would've told her to use something with more stopping power."

He shifted himself around his bad arm and groaned, as if he wanted to distract me. It worked enough to get me to inspect the wound. The slug had been neat going in and hadn't exited. "Can we hold off on the hospital? I don't think bullet holes are covered by my health insurance," he tried weakly.

His reluctance suited me. I didn't want to turn him over to anyone just yet. I followed his directions to the medicine cabinet in the bathroom, for bandages and disinfectant. The cabinet also held things a woman would need, whether or not she'd been shot. But no glossy red lipstick. There was a small tiled shower stall and two jogging outfits draped on the towel rack. On the other side of the bathroom was a library that was being used for something else, with a futon couch unfolded to make a bed and a woman's rumpled sundress laid over a chair. The dress was a size too small for Lupe Jackson.

"Getting your rocks off?" He'd come inside to track me.

"Not exactly."

"What exactly are you doing here, Dyer?"

"I'm on a case."

"That leads you here? To me? Come on."

His skepticism seemed real, and I could share it. Bruce Cady had few enemies as the southwest rep for the Nature

League—a mannered nonprofit dedicated to establishing nature preserves all over the country. But like any man, Cady did have some purposes that were less lofty. Nearly two years ago, he'd lured a woman—the one I didn't want to lose—away from me. Or at least, she'd ended up with him.

"That's Allison's dress," Cady said. "Her jogging outfit. Want to check the underwear?"

"It's hers. I recognize it. You two living here now? What about Lupe Jackson?"

"Is that her name?" He turned and led me into the sparsely furnished office, where the walls were painted like canyons and decorated with large color photographs of wilderness: Zion, Bryce, the Maroon Bells. He closed and locked the door to the street, tugged down a shade over the broken glass, and held out his bad arm. I treated and bandaged it not too tenderly, and again he seemed to load on the grimaces and groans.

"Lupe Jackson, that's what you called her? Don't tell me. She was cheating on her husband, and you suspect me."

"Was she cheating on her husband?"

"I never saw her before."

"You must have. You said she could outrun us."

"I was just going by her appearance, her moves." He licked his lips. "You barge in here right behind a crazy woman who tries to kill me, acting mysterious. You don't have any real authority."

"Only implied. If you don't talk to me, I'll be suspicious, and I'd have to investigate anyway. It's what I do."

"She seemed awfully hot-blooded. Did you hear what she called me?"

"Not all of it, no."

"You were following her. Why?"

He was turning the questions back on me. He had poise, leaning there with a fresh bullet wound and telling me nothing. I could have roughhoused him, but I doubted my motives and with his do-gooder position he'd have powerful allies, for whom Henry Dyer would be so much shoe scrapings. I would work him, but cautiously.

"This is about some stolen falcons," I said.

"You're working for Edwina Garrett?" He read my look. "She and I are old friends. I've been all over her land surveying the wildlife and vegetation. She sits on our board." He sounded strangely bitter. "She told me weeks ago some trespassers might be trying to trap those peregrines—and now it's happened? It was my advice to hire someone to stop it. I never imagined she'd resort to you."

"We all have to resort to something."

"Don't you get it? That's why the Jackson woman came here. She thought Edwina might buy back the falcons and that I'd act as an intermediary. Our association is no secret. I threatened to call the cops, she started shooting." Cady gave me a triumphant look: he had explained his way clear. "So you don't know where the falcons are?"

"You were half right before. Lupe Jackson's husband was involved—he trapped the falcons this morning. But they're missing now. An hour ago Lupe didn't have them, and she acted like she wasn't sure where they were. She also said there was a buyer expecting delivery."

"That couldn't be me, or Edwina. Was she lying?"

"To someone. Maybe she just thought she could hit you up for some quick cash."

"Well, that rules me out," Cady said. "And Edwina, for that matter. She's land rich and cash poor." The bitterness had resurfaced. "She could sell off ten or twenty acres, but she refuses to consider it. Have you seen her house? She might as well be living in a tent. She's determined to donate every last acre to the League. Once she dies, it'll all go over."

"It's her land."

"Yes." He said it between clenched teeth. It was out of character, how her altruism bothered him, and he realized it. He rubbed his bad arm and let out a sigh of pain.

10

Cady decided a hospital was the preferable alternative to my prying. I took him in the Scout. He protected his wound as the stiff suspension found every bump and the open windows let in the hot breeze. We were in the minority among the air-conditioned sedans whose drivers were hidden behind darkly tinted glass. They could have been empty cars operated by remote control. Maybe they all were.

"Weird," Cady said. "You and me getting thrown together like this." He added wryly, "Allison will love it."

"She would."

"You hear we're getting married?"

"Sure. I heard. Let's talk about murder instead." I'd been saving the subject, to spring it on him.

He stared at me and licked his lips. He'd been doing that. People do when they get shot and run low on fluids. They also do it when they get nervous and deceitful. And with some of them it's probably heredity, or environment, or the fault of society.

He let me dredge it up on my own. "Lupe Jackson's husband was named Artie. A few hours ago his throat was cut."

Cady looked shocked and concerned and all the other

things he should have looked while I sketched in the killing. Then he swallowed and licked his lips. "Who did it?"

"Got any ideas?"

"No. Why would I?"

"There's a world of suspects. He was running illegal trap lines and trafficking in wildlife. Killing is what trappers do for a living, even the most ethical ones. And he had some partners who might have wanted to do business without him. Or he could have been double-crossed by the buyer who wanted the falcons, or on something else he had for sale. About the only person who seems clear right now is Lupe Jackson. I just don't see her doing it, and she had her own suspicions."

"She didn't mention them to me. So the cops will be involved."

"Now that there's been a killing, no way around it. And the hospital will report this shooting."

Cady expelled air from his lungs. "This won't be good for me. My ability to do work depends on my image. It has to be spotless. People don't hand over big money and valuable pieces of land to someone linked to a murder investigation."

"I'm not interested in going public either," I said. "Edwina Garrett wanted this handled privately."

He wasn't happy about the prospects. Neither was I.

At the hospital we used the emergency door and got the priority treatment. Within fifteen minutes someone looked at Cady's arm. A half hour later we got a nurse. Eventually we rated a doctor, who had Cady trundled away. While the bullet was being dug out, I phoned my client to bring her up to date, and to ask for permission to mingle with the law, if it came to that. Edwina Garrett didn't answer the rings.

Cady had asked me to hang around, promising he had more to tell me. After all the delays the operation itself was as quick as any knifing. In the room where they wheeled him afterward a higher-echelon nurse tried to drive me out. With

Cady's help and the promise to be brief I prevailed, but not before she made me feel extremely unclean.

"I had them go with a local," Cady said. "This is no time to be knocked out." His cheeks were flushed red against the sheets and there was sweat on his forehead. His hair was still neat. "I get the feeling I'm included in your world of suspects," he said.

"Nobody's excluded."

There was a commotion as a gaunt old man leaned into the room against the complaints of the nurse.

"Oh no," Cady said.

"That you?" the old man called hoarsely. He got past the nurse and over to Cady, holding a fistful of spindly blue wildflowers. "How you doing, *hijo?*" he asked.

"As well as can be expected," Cady said. He introduced us. The old man was his father, Guillermo.

"Good to meet you," Guillermo Cady said as he shook my hand. His was all calluses. He was the vestige of a working-man, his body worn away. What was left was mostly tendons and big veins and loose brown skin and a voice that was only a loud whisper. He walked carefully, as if the next fall could be his last. It was obvious he'd been seriously ill. He had gray stubble on his chin but his gray hair was combed and his eyes were alertly on us. "Nurse called up and said you'd been shot. Maria brought me down. That little girl is good for more than just keeping house. We just packed up the baby and went. She's parking the car."

The old man didn't want to dwell on the help he needed. He thrust out his fistful of flowers. "Here. These'll cure you faster than any doctors will."

"If anyone's an expert on doctors, you are," Bruce Cady said. He accepted the flowers, sparsely leaved stalks that had produced the slender petaled ornaments. They seemed abstract in the sterile room. "*Ipomopsis longiflora:* pale trumpets."

"Got a side yard full of them," Guillermo Cady said. "You know; plants and me, we get along."

"Before he got sick he was a landscaper," Bruce Cady said.

"A gardener," Guillermo Cady said. "A damn good one too."

They were no match, the archaic brown-skinned gardener and his upscale white-skinned son, and there was a tension between them. They were family, and that could have explained it.

"You still got two arms," Guillermo Cady said. "I was worried, but when I heard it was just a twenty-two, I figured, no sweat. A woman's gun. You been fooling around again?"

I was getting mired in them. I had to pull free, before the law arrived, and I told them so.

"Let me finish," Bruce Cady said. "It's essential those peregrines aren't manhandled or treated like so much cargo. The kind of person that would do this . . . The falcons could be ruined for the wild. They might die if they don't get the proper care, and even if they do, sometimes a falcon held like this will just refuse to eat and commit suicide. And the young ones—there are three more in the nest that aren't ready to fly, and they can't feed themselves. They won't last long on their own, especially in this heat. Are you doing anything about them?"

"As soon as I get out of here. I don't like raiding nests, but there doesn't seem to be any option now."

"I'm positive Edwina will consider it part of the job. I'll draw you a map of where the nest is." Cady was using his own job skills, organizing, directing. He got a pencil stub from his father and sketched on the back of the menu that was inflicted on patients. The falcons had nested near the top of the rock cliffs I'd seen at sunrise. Cady told me how to reach the nest by roping down from the top.

"You only have a couple hours of daylight left. You shouldn't try the cliffs alone. I'll have somebody with experience meet you up there. And I'll try to reach Edwina."

"I won't wait for help. I've done enough of that here." I took my scolding and left him with his pale trumpets and his skeleton of a father. There was a uniformed deputy I didn't recognize asking at the nurses' station. I walked the other way, toward the fire stairs, and met a Hispanic woman who seemed too young to be mothering her red-faced baby. She had to be Maria, looking a little frantic in search of her other ward, the old man who was sick with something no one wanted to name. Her baby's cries echoed down the long white hallway.

11

A rough track cut around and up the back side of the cliffs, climbing in and out of national forest, at that elevation dry and dusty with piñon pine and juniper and some bushy oaks. Edwina Garrett had parked in a logged-off spot, in a battered old topless jeep that still had its army paint, complete with the white star on the hood. Another vehicle had been left smack in the sort-of road, a type that I knew all too well: a Game and Fish pickup, a Chevy painted institutional blue, with the quail logo on the door and the flashers in the front grill. I couldn't get past it, though I had an impulse.

I stopped in the clearing and made myself available. A woman got out of the pickup, wearing the tan uniform and the swagger that went with it; she put it on a little heavy for me. A slim whole-milk Anglo with ash blond hair pinned up out of the way, and orange-lensed sunglasses trying to toughen her homespun features. Too pretty, I thought, not for the first time. She had come packing for bear, or men like me, with a Magnum on her cop-style belt. She stood out of my reach.

"Hello, Henry," she said.

"Yes, it's him," Edwina Garrett said. "Now, if you'll get out of the road we'll take it from here."

Allison Crews crossed her arms and leaned against the pickup. She'd been sweating into the Game and Fish shirt.

"Cady had them radio you?" I said. "No need."

"Don't be like that," Allison said.

"Why do you people have to nose into everything?" Edwina Garrett asked.

"You aren't licensed to trap falcons, in the nest or out of it," Allison said. She nodded at me. "And I doubt he is."

Edwina Garrett hawked and spit into the dust. She looked hardy in a short-brimmed Stetson that had been tugged out of shape, a work shirt, high-waisted jeans, and cowboy boots that were one big scuff.

"Don't make a big deal out of it," Allison said. "I have a responsibility here. The department does. I know what I'm doing. Are you going to work out on that rock face?"

"I don't do cliffs," Edwina Garrett said. "He does, though."

Allison chuckled and walked over to the Scout. "What d'you have in here, some of your old gold line?" She reached in the window and fingered my obsolescent climbing rope. "Safer to climb with a buddy. You were my buddy once, Henry."

"All right," I said. "You win. You are the undeniable macho queen of this mountain. Now let's go get the falcons."

She smiled without parting her lips. "We'll take my truck and my gear." She walked back to the Game and Fish pickup and started turning it around.

"That damn boy," Edwina Garrett said. It took me a moment to realize she meant Bruce Cady. "He should never have brought her into this. He's thinking with his balls." She kicked the dirt and focused her imposing stare on me. "You also, I suppose, the way she's acting. So you lost two of my falcons already?"

"I didn't lose them, they got re-stolen."

"And the trespasser's murdered. I won't be mourning Artie Jackson. He's no loss. So it'll botch my privacy and invite in the sheriff and Game and Fish. I'm still not trusting my falcons to any bureaucrats. Keep on it, and don't get sidetracked into solving anything else. I don't care who got rid of Jackson."

"The two crimes will be hard to separate."

"Well, try. Can't you turn up any other angles?"

"A couple."

Edwina Garrett began to cry. Nothing about her face or her composure changed, except now there were tears. I had seen this sudden crying before, in old people who had a lifetime of sorrow to tap. "And Bruce gets shot. Is he all right?"

"He seemed to be."

"Was Guillermo there? He's dying himself. Cancer. It's in his lungs, it's all through him. He was such a strong man."

The Game and Fish pickup was idling in the sort-of road. The horn blared. Edwina Garrett closed down her hard cry. "You heard what I said," she said. "I'll pay for recovering falcons, young ones and adults alike. But not for this other stuff."

I didn't agree to anything. I walked away and climbed into the government truck next to Allison Crews. Edwina Garrett got into her antique jeep. She sat there gripping the steering wheel, exposed to the sun. Allison shifted us into first and let out the clutch and we started to roll.

12

It had gotten late. The sun was riding the Tortolita range off to the west. The cliffs dropped away below us. Allison opened the camper shell on the pickup and shouldered a coil of purple nylon rope, a stylish European braid. She grabbed aluminum trinkets, slings, a small day pack. Close to the edge the ground turned to stone and began to plunge. According to the map Cady had drawn, the falcons had nested on a ledge thirty feet down. I leaned out but couldn't see the ledge or the base of the cliffs. The cactus and mesquite in the valley were minute. Allison jangled as she hopped onto a massive boulder slanting out over the emptiness.

"You up to this?" she asked.

"Ah reckon so," I said, using my codger's accent.

"Same old Henry. You've got a few years to go. I'll rappel down first and scout it out."

"Same old Allison. Man better go second."

She made a face, then doubled the rope around a thick juniper back from the edge and heaved the coil out past me. It fell out of sight and slapped against the rock face. She wound a nylon strap around herself, made a seat, and cinched it between her legs with a harness of carabiners—aluminum O-rings—and brake bars. She fed the rope through the brake bars and around her hips and backed toward the edge, controlling the feed with her right hand, testing the slippage. Satisfied, she shouldered into the pack and pulled on leather gloves and an orange watchman's cap so her hair wouldn't snag in the brake bars. She tossed me gear.

"Here." She was mad about that crack about her and men. The sling around her waist and rump accentuated her figure, which was worth accentuating, but she didn't want to hear about that, either.

She backed over the edge and let the rope hold her, standing perpendicular to the rock, studying the way below, jumped sideways and let out some rope and dropped a few yards, landing lightly with her boots against the vertical rock. She did this again, and again.

From below rose a piercing cry, and another. The food cry of the young falcons: the eyases in their aerie. At least some of them were alive to be hungry. They were accustomed to five or six meals a day, fresh meat delivered around sunrise and sunset, the peak times of hunting.

The falcons cried over the valley. From the aerie they had a view, and they were protected somewhat from the nest raiders: fox, coyote, the other mammals and birds that could only try sneaking in when the adults weren't around. Up by the Salt River I'd seen a lone male peregrine drive off a full-grown eagle three times its size, and that eagle was glad to get away.

Allison had dropped below the overhang. I clambered along the drop-off, trying for a better vantage, and came upon the falcons' kitchen. A litter of feathers and regurgitated bones and claws and gristly body parts had collected below a gnarled oak limb that made a good perch. The adults on their feverish parental feed would have sat here and plucked their prey, tenderizing it for the young. Peregrines kill just about anything on the wing, from a goose on down.

The cry from below had changed to the *kek-kek* alarm call.

"I can see them," Allison yelled. "All three."

I got back to where the purple rope dived over the edge, rigged myself a sling, snapped on carabiners.

"I'm off the rope," Allison yelled. "Come ahead."

The rope had gone slack. I looped it here and grabbed it there and backed over the drop-off, kicked off the rock face, dropped, kicked again, dropped. The rock was smooth and limestoney, relatively friendly. There were seams and creases and crevices. Past the overhang I swung free until I could get down to where the rock angled toward me again. The *kek-kek*-ing was louder and more intense, below and off to the left. Allison was over there, sitting on a narrow ledge with her back to the rock and her legs dangling. I worked the rope and the rock and swung over. As I knew she would, she started with the orders.

"Careful." The ledge was about twenty inches wide, slanting down slightly beyond her, tapering to nothing. The three adolescent falcons had crowded toward the far end. They looked to be about four weeks old, nearly full grown, with most of their cottony down already replaced by finely patterned feathers. Their talons and beaks were fully developed, and they had the outlaw's mask around the uncompromising peregrine glare.

"We'll do this slowly. They're a week or two away from flying. We don't want to scare them into trying too soon." She slid sideways on the ledge and I got my balance standing next to her, fed enough rope past my brake bar so I could turn around and sit down. The rock against my back was warm. The sun was setting on the horizon in front of us, behind the far jagged Tortolitas. At most we had an hour of twilight.

"Tie yourself off." I got it done, doubling the rope through my carabiner so we wouldn't lose it, or me. She worked without a belay, talking to the falcons, introducing herself, sliding closer to them, leaving her pack next to me. Except for the coating of droppings, the ledge was clean; there wasn't any mess of feathers and vomited bones like there had been up in the kitchen. Some peregrines keep a clean aerie, some don't; each one makes up its own mind. The ledge was also uncluttered by twigs and the other doodads most birds use to make a comfy nest. Peregrines don't bother: when the time comes to lay eggs, they just scrape out a little spot in rock and dirt. The only comfort the young ones have growing up is in their own ferocity.

"Don't move." The falcons huddled together hissing and screaming as she reached over them gingerly and dropped her hat on the wisp of ledge. The flacons were cornered then, between her and the hat.

"Get ready with a bag." Inside the pack were three black cotton sacks that could be closed by drawstrings. I flopped one open. Allison tried to arch her outside arm around the falcons and herd them toward her. She was still telling them things. When she made a move for the closest one the other two threw themselves on their backs and raked out with their talons. There was a lot of peregrine noise and loose tufts of down. I held open the sack and she thrust in the first struggling falcon, I cinched the drawstrings on her forearms, she slid out her gloved hands, I finished closing the sack. The falcon calmed immediately, the old falconry principle: if it can't see, it won't fight. She grabbed another one and we bagged it separately. The third one had learned something and it jumped upright and spread its wings and shuffled away clumsily on talons intended for perching and ripping, and I thought it might leap over the edge. At the last instant Allison caught it by one leg and around the body and thrust it into the third sack. She grinned. Her hair was coming loose. She'd been scratched on one wrist and a cheek and was bleeding a little.

"I felt them," she said. "They're beautiful."

There wasn't enough room on the ledge for me to reasonably arrange the falcons in their sacks. They were heavy for their size and wouldn't fit in the pack we had.

"We'll have to tie the sacks to us when we go up," she said.

"All right."

The twilight had expanded around us. The colors were coming out, subtle pinks and greens that had been lurking in the pale stone. Soon everything would fade into night. Allison jangled her gear, realigning her sling, hooking up an ascending ratchet. I was still managing not to look straight down.

A big rock fell past us, bounding off the cliff face, and then another one, tumbling down and down.

"Hey," a voice shouted out from above. "Hey, you fuckers down there." I couldn't see past the overhang, but I could tell it was a man up there, a big angry man.

13

He wanted the young falcons. He yelled for them. "Yoo-hoo . . . yoo-hoo. Send up the birds. Willing to spend the night down there? Or the rest of your lives?" He lifted the rope, yanked me off the ledge. Allison grabbed me and pulled me back. He yanked the rope again, whipping the slack against the rock face. "Yoo-hoo . . . yoo-hoo."

"Maniac," Allison said. "Friend of yours?"

He started singing, "Send up the falcons, the falcons, the falcons."

"Can you see him?" she asked.

"No. Where's your gun?"

"In the pickup. Yours?"

"Same place."

"Hey," he yelled. "I want some action, or I'm gonna cut this rope and push this fish cop's truck over the edge and the hell with you."

"We could wait him out," I said. "Somebody will come searching for us."

We looked at each other.

"That isn't so good, either," Allison said. "He might throw Edwina over the edge too."

"Maybe he's bluffing."

"Hey, you fuckers," he yelled. "Watch out below." The

spare tire from the Game and Fish pickup bounded down the rock past us. Then the flashers from the front grill crashing and spinning down; he must have torn them loose. Then he started firing pistols that sounded like ours. Bullets careened off the rock. We were protected by the overhang—unless he changed positions. He'd already changed one thing: *yoo-hoo* to *yee-haw*.

"I'm going up," Allison said.

"Be serious."

"This is my operation. It's my truck he's destroying."

"If anyone's going up, it's me." She ignored me, tying the bagged falcons to her sling. "He sounds big," I told her. "I'll go first, and you sneak up and surprise us."

"I'll surprise you," she said, and she leapt over me and caught the rope and knocked us both off the ledge. We swung down and sideways as a pendulum, scraping against the rock. I was still tied to the rope, and it stretched and caught us. She kicked and climbed off me. I was hanging from my carabiner. She clung to the rope above me, busy with her ascending ratchet.

"Whatcha doing down there?" With the rope taut we were directly below him. He tugged on the rope. "I got fish cops on the line."

Allison started ratcheting up the rope. The falcons in their sacks dangled off her. I didn't have any fancy ratchet. I started up the hard way, hand over hand, walking the rock. It was painful and slow and got more so. I was trying to pull myself out of the depths of middle age.

The light was fading. Allison grunted and scraped and kicked rock fragments down on me as she crested the overhang.

"I got a lady fish cop. Yee-haw." They started fighting, the blows thudding softly. Under the overhang I lost the rock and twisted freely, dizzily. Above the overhang there were traces of handholds and the rock wasn't as strictly vertical.

He poked his head over the top. "I got another one on the line, but he's ugly." Then the son of a bitch cut the rope.

The rock slid by me. I was going down. The hell I was. I hugged it and fingered into it and scraped it with my boots and got myself and the trembling stopped, and then I began to muscle my way up. The son of a bitch had pulled back his head. I heard them fighting again, him huffing and little cries of effort from her. No more sounds, and then his head poked out again, just above me, and I reached up and grabbed him, got him around the neck, and either we were both going all the way to the bottom or he was going to haul me up. He stood up, taking all my weight, and it didn't faze him. He really was big. He slapped me off onto the slanting rock along the edge and tromped for me until I got hold of his leg and then he loosened my head with openhanded swats. He was fighting like a grizzly bear—he was about that size. I couldn't do anything with his leg. He kicked me off and gave me time to get up. He was Reed One or Reed Two, half of the giants in the photo with dead Artie Jackson. The other half didn't seem to be around. Allison was on the ground ten feet away. She had dropped the sacks of falcons over by the truck, where they were wriggling. She was rickety standing up. Reed looked at her, then at me.

"I'll take you both," he said. "Yee-haw."

He lumbered toward me. I picked up a branch and slammed him in the knee. I picked up a rock and smashed it into the center of his chest. I ran across one of the guns and snapped the trigger at him; it was empty. Allison had her belt off and was whipping him with it, the buckle cutting his head and hands as he shielded himself and grabbed the belt and yanked her into him. I moved in with the gun and clubbed his head, his neck, his arms, and he picked me up and lobbed me some distance. I got up, but the one leg wasn't good. He watched me unsnap my carabiners and slip them over my hands to make metal knuckles. I started slamming him, and Allison moved in with her belt again. He took it a long while. He was a son of a bitch, but he wasn't fast, and there were two of us and he'd been kind of lackadaisical about the fight. Allison whipped me too and uttered the little cries with each swing; we were all tangled up and moving in the darkness. Finally the son of a bitch went down. He lay there and made a sound like giggling. Somehow he was getting up. Allison dropped the belt and wandered away. "Thanks a lot," I said. I was sucking air. Shivering. I watched him rise up and surround me. "Come on," I said. Then Allison shot him with the Magnum. The flames lit us up and she shot him again. He twisted away from us and she shot a third time. He pitched forward over the edge and disappeared. She had killed the son of a bitch.

14

It was quiet after the big man went over. Allison drifted to the edge and looked down. Too dusky to see anything, but she lingered there. She came back past me to the Game and Fish pickup, opened the door, laid her pistol on the seat and tried her voice on the radio. Her voice was low, even, polite. The radio was not working. Other things seemed to be broken. She tried the ignition, then got out and lifted the hood of the truck.

"The battery's gone," she said.

She began to collect the gear that littered the ground. Her hat. Her gloves. The sunglasses he'd knocked off her. Things he had ripped off or out of the truck. She picked up each item carefully and placed it in the truck.

"You don't have to do that," I said.

"Shut up," she said. She kept on doing it. She hadn't taken off her rappeling sling, and her carabiners and trinkets still jangled as she moved.

I limped off into the woods, circled, and found what I thought would be there: the big man's transportation. It was a stripped-down Dodge flatbed, mid sixties. The bed was missing, the frame exposed from the cab to the rear bumper, a chewed section of telephone pole. The cab was beaten on the outside, the windshield cracked, and there was a coat hanger loop for an antenna. The inside was grimy, dirt and trash on the floor, and it smelled of rotted meat. A cheap blanket cover was strapped over the bench seat, which had sprung under the big man's weight. There was no key in the ignition, no floor mats under which one might have been hidden, and no guts to the glove box, just shreds of the cardboard liner. Without a flashlight I couldn't look any further. I walked back through the woods. My leg was a little better.

She had everything straightened up. "We have to hike these falcons down off this mountain," she said. She had them lined up in their bags. She fussed with her pack. "This water bottle is leaking. It's been leaking for six months. The seam split and I never did a damn thing about it."

I kept it simple. "His truck is over there. I might be able to start it. I need a screwdriver."

She lugged out the toolbox from her pickup and shuffled through the tools and then just stared at them. "This one," I said, and took a screwdriver, and she followed me and I hot-wired the flatbed truck. In slow motion she had climbed into the cab and was keeping it going with the gas pedal. I got in the passenger side. She sat there pumping the gas, pumping the gas.

"Let's go," I said. She did nothing. I got out and went around to her side and nudged her over, drove us back to the pickup, loaded the falcons in her side. She held one of the sacks on her lap gingerly. I started us down the road. The old Dodge had loose body parts the clapped as we negotiated the bumps.

"He was a son of a bitch," I said. "He cut the rope on me."

She stared straight ahead. "I kept firing. It was so loud. Usually I have the earmuffs on. I hope he went all the way to the bottom. Otherwise it might be difficult, finding him."

I stopped the truck and pulled her out. She was pliable. I hugged her, and the memory of her.

"He had it coming," I said.

She fit me like before, tall enough to see over my shoulder.

"Henry." She clutched me. "Henry." Too quickly, she stiffened. "Get back in the truck."

"He had it coming," I said again. I released her and we assumed our positions in the truck. We lurched ahead.

"Two heads on one body, that was always our problem," she said.

"It's been a while."

"And it'll be a while longer."

We rode some more listening to the truck banging itself.

"I never pulled the trigger on anyone before," she said. "It's my case now."

"Mine too. That makes it our case."

"Just keep your distance. And don't get in my way."

"I learned that years ago."

"I had to teach you."

"You thought you had to. Okay, okay. I saw what happened to the last man who got in your way. And we didn't even get his number."

She looked at me. "It was One or Two. Of course you know every weirdo in southern Arizona, the Reeds included."

"I know of them. What are they, punk rednecks?"

The talk was bringing her out of it, and job talk was safer for both of us. She shrugged. "Game and Fish has a file on Artie Jackson; the Reeds are in there, dishonorable mention. We had all three of them down as dirty. They were helping Jackson take lizards on the T and E list"—she meant threatened and endangered—"for collectors and dealers back east. Anything that's scarce, people want. Some of what's dealt winds up laundered, sent to museums and schools. Jackson did snakes, too. Ridgenose rattlers are up to a hundred and a half wholesale. Mainly he was into skins: bobcat, anything else he could trap or shoot. Or for a couple hundred he'd take somebody out after lion or bear. Like you used to. Only the places and times he went, it wasn't a sport. It was an industry, illegal as hell. Seasons, permits—he didn't bother."

"One visit to his place and I could see that. What were you waiting for?"

"You know how it is. We don't have enough people to work half of what's out there. Anybody we bust gets fined a couple hundred bucks and goes right back to whatever he was doing before we got interested. The laws have no punch and judges get confused when we bring in a real case, like we should be out ticketing kids who are two catfish over the limit instead. Public must feel the same way. And the feds at Fish and Wildlife only get involved when it's twenty-nine guys in an eight-state conspiracy. You're the one who left the department. Remember why?"

"You're reminding me."

"We were tracking Jackson, and we'd have taken him off soon, but we wanted to get the Reeds at the same time and they made it tough—no schedule, no address. Real shadowy. Phantoms of the desert. Your kind, Henry."

"It was One who rousted us. Two has facial scars."

"One was plenty for me."

"For us, you mean. Any idea where Scarface is?"

"No, and I wouldn't tell you if I had. We can share the basics, but when this case is cracked I'll be holding the hammer. With his brother dead, Reed Two is my prime suspect. Both of them together must have killed Jackson and picked up the falcons. They weren't satisfied and had to come back for the babies too."

"You work these kinds of investigations?"

"Sometimes. I'm working this one."

"Is that wise?"

"What?"

"Considering your personal connection."

"What connection?"

"Bruce Cady."

"He's a victim, not a suspect. My feelings for Bruce won't interfere if yours don't."

"Sure. You can grill him at the wedding. When is it?"

She took her time answering, her eyes glinting from the dash lights. "Two days, if he's out of the hospital, and he expects to be. We would have done it months ago if we'd had the money."

"Now do you?"

"Bruce has been doing some consulting on the side."

"What sort of consulting?"

"Are we making small talk? I don't get that idea." One of the falcons interrupted, fluttering in its bag and then settling down. "He's a good man," she said. "The places he's had a hand in preserving . . . He's making a contribution that will be felt for generations to come. And he sacrifices to do it. The Nature League pays him next to nothing. He's even had to give up his apartment and move into his office. Any money he gets goes to keep his father alive."

"I'll ask again: what sort of consulting?"

She huffed in exasperation. "He's a biologist. He does environmental assessments, wildlife and plant surveys of areas that are going to be developed. Mostly he's subcontracting with the county, when the planning staff can't handle it. They're overloaded by all this crazy growth."

"He do anything up at Desierto Lindo?"

"I think he did. Why?"

"Artie Jackson had a clipping about the place on his bulletin board, marked with exclamation points."

"So ha ha. Jackson was thinking of retiring, and he didn't want to go to the old trappers' home."

We reached the clearing where we'd left Edwina Garrett in her antiquated jeep. No sign of her or the jeep.

"Reed must have missed her," I said.

"She could have taken him," Allison said.

My Scout was nosed off to the side. It hadn't been tampered with. We neatened up, using water from the jug in back.

"You should think about your own personal connections and where they're taking you," she said. "You're acting like you want to bust Bruce."

"His story doesn't quite make sense. Lupe Jackson didn't have to shoot him to get away. If we're talking about women who can take men, she could have taken him easy. She didn't need the gun at all, unless she was settling some score."

"Like what?"

"I don't know. She ran right at him after Artie was killed."

"And then you carefully waited outside until she shot him."

"I just wanted to see what she was up to."

"As you like to say, Henry, sure. Wise up. You're still blaming Bruce for my leaving you."

"I'm trying not to blame anyone."

"I was just tired of butting heads. You and me are too much alike, and it took me too long to realize it, and I don't want to relive it now. You should back off this investigation."

"I'm allergic to backing off. There'll be enough to investigate to keep all of us busy."

She sighed angrily, shook her head. "Don't you come after Bruce, or I'll come after you."

"Sounds good."

"Not that way," she said.

15

We made a caravan down to the highway, Allison driving the flatbed and me the Scout. At the junction she stopped, aiming north toward Edwina Garrett's place, where she could drop off the young falcons and phone in the report of the shooting.

I pulled in beside her and leaned over my rolled-down window. "I can't get hung up here hunting the body and taking cement casts of every footprint and tire track. Tell the sheriff's people I'll be in later tonight to see the detectives."

"You better back me up on this."

"I will. But this is your element. And there's another chore I don't mind leaving for the department. Artie Jackson had some maps in a drawer; I think they showed the location of his trap lines. Somebody will have to check it out."

"I'll do it," she said with disgust. "In the morning." She knew what I was getting at. Somebody would have to run the trap lines and either let loose or finish off whatever had been caught. With the standard leg-hold traps, most of the animals would be crippled. They'd have to be killed.

"This is getting violent. Be careful," Allison said. "So long."

We pulled out, going in opposite directions, the same old story. I thought about that, and about the nasty trap-line chore, and the two missing falcons around which the case seemed to be spinning. With people being murdered around them, the falcons could become a liability, incriminating evidence that had to be destroyed. I tried to see the case through their eyes. We were all sons of bitches to them. Or meat.

Somebody'd left a hot lite beer under the seat and I resorted to it. Miles later the first sheriff's car went by, running its lights, trying to look as wicked as any trouble it might find. But there were far more wicked and larger troubles lurking.

Dyer, here's to *Falco peregrinus*. The predator supreme, and a symptom of all our screwups. No creature was ever swifter or deadlier. Evolved to hunt other birds on the wing, diving after prey, they've been timed in excess of two hundred and forty miles an hour. Such perfection. And such an affront to us Homo sapiens, the heavy walkers.

Of course our first response was, put peregrines to work, make them hunt for us, and for centuries of early falconry in Europe and other cradles of civilization they were the noble-man's bird of choice. Then technology rolled, we could hunt with gunpower instead—so much more efficient, if less artful—and suddenly we had to compete against peregrines for the same pigeons and ducks and partridges, so we turned our guns on the peregrines too, put a bounty on them, blew them away by the thousands. We got very efficient rigging fence posts and other likely perches with leg-hold traps, so any peregrine landing would be caught and exhaust itself against the steel and die dangling upside down. We tried for maximum efficiency and even went a little mad about pere-grines, made a fad out of looting their nests for the eggs, pretty things, mottled red and white and no two alike, and so we had to possess them, and hoard them away in museums or on living room mantels or in cigar boxes in somebody's uncle's attic.

Lousy egg suckers.

Have another swig of hot lite beer, Dyer. That's what the world offers. Stories like Wild Horse Charlie used to tell, about how even the war against Hitler turned into a war against peregrines. It seems homing pigeons were standard equipment aboard some British aircraft, so pilots who ditched at sea could send back their location, and somebody got the idea that a peregrine might hunt a pigeon somewhere and maybe leave a pilot stranded. So the British government hired ranks of hit men to try to exterminate all the peregrines and wreck the aeries, in the name of the bugaboo "national security."

But through all this the peregrine managed to hang on, until it got done in by some overeducated fools.

Here's to overeducated fools. The ones who came up with DDT and the sister chlorinated hydrocarbons, may they sip of their own poisonous and most efficient nectar. It got into the peregrines, working its way up the food chain to the top predators, and hit them right where it could do the most damage: screwed up their hormones, made them too sick to breed; they lost interest, or they laid eggs that didn't hatch, the shells too thin, too fragile, some glitch in calcium production. They'd crush their own eggs sitting on them in the nest and wind up eating the remains—a natural response, wouldn't you say?

Anything wrong with your reproductive urge lately, Dyer? We're atop the food chain too, and cynicism might not save us.

After the big die-off, ten, fifteen years ago, there were no peregrines left in this country east of the Mississippi. In the West we had maybe fifty pair. They were sparse or extinct all over Europe, and thinning out in Canada, Australia, Siberia, Japan. They've made a little comeback since DDT's been banned, but other countries still use DDT by the ton, most of it made in this country, and the peregrines here pick it up in the winter when they migrate to Mexico and South America, or right at home eating other birds that migrate. And the new generation of pesticides and toxics is coming in, and after that there'll be another generation, and another, and peregrines are going to be sensitive because that's the kind of species they are.

And now we have to put up with this happy news about how captive breeding is saving the peregrine, raising them in cages and releasing them in places where pesticide residues aren't too high, so we have peregrines showing up back east again, nesting not on their usual cliffs and canyon walls but on skyscraper ledges in Boston and Baltimore and New York, and in the West among the steel and glass towers in downtown Denver and Phoenix. But the news is not quite complete, no good news ever is, and downtown with its shitty air and shitty water and half dead prey will never replace all the peregrine habitat that's been lost or corrupted. Captive breeding by itself will never bring about a recovery of the species; look at the odds. Peregrines are loner birds. Any particular male and female might not hit it off in captivity, they might fight, the female might kill the male—it rarely goes the other way—or they might tolerate each other but not mate, or breed but lay no eggs, or they might lay eggs that were infertile. And any peregrines that are hatched and released have an even higher mortality than ones raised in the wild. Not surprising, is it? Peregrines live by the hunt, not an easy way to make a living, and they need every edge they can get. In the wild even in the best conditions only 20, 25 percent survive to breed. They get shot, poisoned, blown out of the nest by storms, eaten by owls while they're sleeping; some of them just starve because they are consistently a fraction of a second too slow on the kill, and they can't make it up. Everything has to click just right for the peregrine, and does that sound like the world we are making?

This is lousy beer and the worst part is you can get used to it.

Consume, Dyer. We are the consumers. Doubling in population every couple of decades now, and in the long run what does that mean for the peregrine, or any other species for that matter? And with falconry fashionable again, we're back going after wild peregrines because there aren't enough captive-bred birds available, or we just prefer ones from the wild. So the total pressure increases. Any comeback peregrines are managing, it could just as easily go the other way, and it probably will sooner or later. Hell, some subsistence cultures are still raiding peregrine nests and eating the unfledged young.

Don't spread that around, Dyer, or peregrine will wind up on the menu in these yuppified new-cuisine cafés. Better shut up or it'll be *le peregrine* beside a sprig of parsley for sure.

16

Tucson's lights spread out below the dark mountains. I went down into them, to a house on the west side, a one-story brick in an old desert neighborhood with more character than what they're making now. It had an acre and a third. Apartments had sprung up next door, two and three stories tall amidst immature landscaping, leaking noises from TVs and CDs and FM-AM.

Krasner answered my knock, an overwrought fatless little man with slicked-back hair and sideburns in the Chicago style and a sulking face. He did money counseling and didn't have to conform. He was barely dressed in ragged cutoffs and a black leather glove that sheathed his right arm to the elbow. On the glove stood a little hawk.

"Dyer," he said nervously. "Say hello to Lizzie." He dipped his glove and the doorway filled as the hawk unfurled its wings.

"Lizzy?"

"Borden. I get so bored by all these hawks named Havoc or Fury or Vengeance. Let me show a little more wit."

"How you doing, Lizzie," I said.

The hawk retracted its wings and rode Krasner's arm into the living room, which was decorated like a large and elegant birdcage: a couple of vinyl-covered footstools on a red concrete floor, dim light emanating from a flex lamp facing the wall, violins from a stereo deployed on the floor. Hanging from the pitched ceiling on chrome chains was a chrome trapeze bar. Nothing else except, in the far corner, a swatch of green indoor-outdoor carpeting fertilized by bird droppings and sprouting a welded steel perch.

Krasner approached the perch and persuaded the hawk to hop on. It was a long-tailed Cooper's hawk, smaller than a peregrine, with a sharp look obscured somewhat by the summer molt: blue-gray back, muted orange chest, red eyes. Last year's feathers had faded. The new ones growing in were bright.

The hawk let Krasner tie its legs to an intricate leash of jesses, swivel rings, and elastic that was secured to the perch. The hawk had limited movement. It shuffled back and forth on the perch, finding a position. Krasner told it, "Easy."

He sat down on one of the footstools, his back straight. Then he stood up, shoved his hands in his back pockets.

"Last time you were flying Teddy Roosevelt," I said.

"He's on his own now; I let him go. No more Harris hawks for me. They're too verbal, real screamers. Never had one that knew when to shut up. Not like Lizzie here."

Lizzie roused, ruffling her feathers, smoothing them out. She pulled up one leg and balanced on the other one.

"She'll last about ten minutes," Krasner said. "Then she'll give the jesses a try. Won't you, Lizzie?"

Lizzie screwed her head upside down and stared at us. "She's wondering about you," Krasner said. "Sign of intelligence. A Cooper's is smart compared to a Harris. More personality too. But jumpy."

"The traits go together."

"Right. Lots of people don't want the hassle of a Cooper's. I say birds are what you make of them."

"Where'd you get her?"

"Nest down by the Santa Ritas." Krasner was a licensed falconer, and Cooper's hawks weren't protected. "You after me for something? That's the way you're coming off. You been in a fight?"

"I'm working on peregrines."

Krasner slid one hand through his hair. "Don't have much use for them. Peregrines man too easy." He meant the birds took too readily to falconry, and men. "Like a Harris. A Harris will just about train itself. In two weeks, you can have one killing for you. That's why they're so popular. A Harris will make a bad falconer look good, and make a good falconer look great. A Cooper's gives you an exact reading."

"I can tell you're hooked on Lizzie. What about peregrines? Know anybody who's into them?"

Krasner started pacing. "No one with any sense. Let's put aside the acquisition problem; they're hard to come by, but not impossible. What you have with peregrines is a specialized form of hunting that makes it difficult to participate—the name itself, peregrine, is Latin for 'wanderer.' They're all over the sky, go ten, fifteen miles or more on a kill, and maybe they'll come back and maybe not. They'll chase after anything that's flying, and disdain anything on the ground, whereas a Cooper's or a Harris will crash down on a rabbit or a squirrel or a jogging quail. Unless it's an emergency, a peregrine won't—maybe if there's a grounded bird a peregrine will go aerobatic, trying to strafe it, spook it into taking off where it can be hit. And no matter how much you torque one down, keep it hungry thinking you and dinner go together, a peregrine is always on the verge of saying bye-bye."

"You said they manned pretty easily."

"They get used to you, they accept you, yes. And they pick up the fundamentals. But they can blow you off just as quickly. Maybe it's just that everything is superfluous to them, except the hunt. That's what the people who fly peregrines say. You can't just fly a peregrine off the fist, you've got to build it up into this ritual, make a performance out of it. You stand around while the peregrine rings up, you know, doing the tight spirals, until it reaches its pitch. Then it waits on, while you look around for something to flush.

You've got to use a dog or beat the bushes yourself to scare up a pigeon or something, and once it's flying the peregrine might finally get interested, stoop and smack it down. You're working for the bird, and the whole thing is a show, rigged—compared to a peregrine, that pigeon is in slow motion. But that stoop to the kill, that's the rush, the ego trip. And it all fits in with the history of the bird, the prestige, how aristocrats flew them and all. The sport of kings, all that phony crap. Peregrines are arrogant birds for arrogant people. I wouldn't have one."

"Who would?"

Krasner didn't answer right away. There aren't many falconers; they tend to be clannish, huddled by their peculiar hobby, but to one another they gossip. I was counting on it.

"You asked that before," Krasner said. "You're doing some hunting yourself, aren't you?"

"I don't know who yet."

Krasner jumped up and grabbed the trapeze, hung there and studied me. The hair under his arms was as slick as his hairdo. The violins played on.

"That time you went out with me and Teddy Roosevelt," Krasner said. "You liked it?"

"Yes."

"So why do you want to come down on anybody in falconry?"

"If I do, it'll be somebody breaking the regs. Giving all of you a bad name."

Krasner smiled sharply. He chinned himself, did a roll and wound up sitting on the bar. Down on the perch, Lizzie the hawk put down the foot she'd tucked against her belly. She shook herself again and seemed to tighten her feathers.

"She's on the edge," Krasner said.

Lizzie craned her head this way at us, then that way. She turned around on her perch and faced the wall.

"This isn't anything against falconry," I said. "I have a specific interest in anyone who might be wanting to buy a peregrine for just about any price, and who wouldn't care if it was taken illegally from the wild."

"Some people only want them from the wild."

"Those are people I want to get to know."

"The cops wouldn't be able to get this. Your old chums at Game and Fish, their snitches have sold everything they know three times over."

Idly, Krasner started to swing. "Peregrines can be an obsession. And they are the loudest birds. One will deafen you in six months."

He dropped to the concrete. Lizzie the hawk turned around on her perch and glared at us.

"I figure, you fly with me, I can help you out a little. I heard about a guy who might fit," Krasner said. "He flies a captive-bred peregrine. A while back he was asking around about improving his stock. Money was mentioned, no amount, but the impression was, enough to overcome any legal objections. He's a Saudi, over here to attend the university. Drives a black Corvette all summer in the desert. He apprenticed with a guy I know."

Krasner padded over to the stereo and picked up a cordless phone it had been hiding. "Arabs get off on what a peregrine can do," he said. "I think it's because they're culturally repressed." He tapped out a number and had a brief conversation. He put the phone down.

"Al Burabi. He'll be flying his bird tomorrow morning. Early." Krasner told me where. "Leave me out of it."

"Thanks."

"Like you said, this sort of crap gives us all a bad name."

Lizzie the hawk spread her wings. She pulled them in, raked the room with her eyes, and spread her wings again.

"Time's up," Krasner said.

The little hawk hurled herself off the perch, as if she intended to fly straight out of sight. She hit the end of the leash, jerked back and down onto the square of green carpet. She leapt against the leash again, and then again, fluttering mightily. Bating is what they call it. Yanked down by the legs a third time, she fluffed her feathers, looked around, and hopped back on the perch.

"She'll be okay now," Krasner said. "Won't you, Lizzie?" He went over and scratched the hawk's chest. "They have so much energy, they have to burn it off. You have to burn it out of them, the idea they can go somewhere." Krasner worked his fingers around the back of the hawk's neck. Lizzie blinked her red eyes, then closed them.

"Not many Coopers will let you do this," Krasner said. "Lovely Lizzie. Hey, when are you coming out with us? Bring Allison too. She liked old Teddy, didn't she? I never saw him accept any stranger like he did her."

"She's with somebody else now."

"Too bad. So come alone. You should see this little girl in action. Right off the fist; I don't have to prep her, she just goes. We work the brush, where a bigger bird wouldn't be any good. She'll zing off into a hackberry, she'll be half flying, half running through fifteen, twenty feet of hackberry, and she'll flush a quail out the other side and keep going until she gets it. She'll chase one right down a gopher hole. Won't you, Lizzie?"

The hawk opened her eyes and aimed them at me.

"She's like a little heat-seeking missile," Krasner said. "She doesn't talk much, though."

17

A police helicopter choppered noisily a quarter mile to the east, probing down with its searchlight, a man-made bird of prey. It raced overhead and lit me up standing on Krasner's driveway and then swung off farther west. Nevertheless, it was about time I turned myself in.

I drove the fringe of the west side to the Pima County Sheriff's Office, a ramshackle complex of mobile homes converted into offices and stuck onto the original building as the law-and-order budget got strained by the downside of the Sun Belt boom.

The station appeared deserted at that hour, but there was a side door where I knew I'd get service. I talked my way back to see Sixto DeGuerra, and then regretted it. He took my arm and walked me. "Buddy, you look like mashed potatoes. We got a bulletin out on you. And a certain somebody here's got a killer bee up her ass."

He took me into a windowless interrogation room and went out and came back with another plainclothes detective, a woman I didn't know, Garbers, and I began to regret everything.

The light from the fluorescent fixtures was harsh. There was only a table missing some of its wood-grain veneer, metal folding chairs, streaked linoleum, and white Sheetrock walls that had been used to take fingerprints.

Garbers turned on a tape recorder. "Time for a little Q and A," she said. "Questions, and arrest." She was big enough leaning over me, with her cinder block face and mortared hair, vanilla golf shirt tucked into never-wrinkle tan slacks, pointed cowboy boots. State of the art in liberated homicide detectives.

"Just how many bodies you racked up today?" she asked.

"Two," I said. "Not counting the walking wounded."

DeGuerra laughed shortly. He had sat down across from me, round and dark with aluminum hair, dressed like Garbers, but less precisely. He tended to primary colors, all at the same time. "I told you he's basically honest."

"I knew there was somebody," Garbers said.

"After midnight we dispense with the formalities," De-Guerra said. He imitated a police siren.

Garbers stared at him, then turned it on me. "Why'd you do Artie Jackson?"

"Do what to him?"

"You were there."

"That's right." I told them what they needed to know.

"Birds?" DeGuerra said. "You're sleuthing for birds?" He laughed. Garbers laughed.

"Hot on the trail of a bird-napper," Garbers said.

They laughed some more.

I said, "Go ahead. I've been adding up reasons all day for you to want me. If this is all you can muster, I couldn't ask for better."

Garbers got in my face. "You're a real smoothie, aren't you?" She did a good job of sneering. "Maybe you pushed Jackson too far trying to get him to fork over these birds. Maybe you aren't as good with a razor knife as you used to be. Maybe your hand slipped. We'd understand."

"Sure," I said. "That's more like it. And then I called nine-one-one to report the body just to make the chase more exciting."

Garbers shrugged. "We don't know it was you called in. Even if you did, could be just to look good, to throw us off."

"Especially when I don't identify myself. To really throw you off, I could have brought the body in on horseback wearing a Nixon mask. Then you wouldn't know what to think."

"The razor's wiped clean, no prints, no witnesses," Garbers said. "Except you, and you didn't see anything."

"*Basta*," DeGuerra said. Garbers gave me a little space. DeGuerra lodged his hands behind his hair, spread his elbows, stretched. He didn't get any bigger.

"We talked to Cady," he said. "Got the story about how you'd come right from the scene of the murder to his place. He didn't go out of his way to exonerate you. We got the impression he wouldn't mind seeing you locked up for a while."

"Nice fellow," Garbers said.

"On the other hand," DeGuerra said, "we got the pickup. Jackson's, the one you say his killer drove off in. A trooper patrolling the Catalina Highway found it abandoned in the ditch. It hadn't been there ten minutes before, so we got the time fixed, and it had to be dumped about when you were downtown letting Cady get shot by Jackson's widow. You couldn't have been both places at once."

"Not even you," Garbers said.

"Of course, anybody could have driven the pickup out there," DeGuerra went on. "Could have been any old car thief, before or after the murder."

"It wasn't. It jibes with what I told you."

"It also jibes with you seeing the truck's gone and you incorporate it in your story." DeGuerra smiled. "You could do it." He held the smile until it was the only thing going in the room and then he let it go. "But this time I don't think you did. This time we got the Reeds."

"Head bashers," Garbers said. "That's all."

DeGuerra smiled again. "They skewered three bikers in a

bar fight last year. With pool cues. It was all they had to work with. We'll go with the Reeds for now."

"And let your buddy here off," Garbers said.

"For now," DeGuerra said. He stood up. It was hard to tell. He came around the table and poked me on the arm. "You took care of half the problem for us, you and that blonde you used to run around with. We wait long enough, maybe you'll take care of the other half."

"Reed Two? Could be I'm not interested in him."

"Afraid he's going to get his own head bashed. Again," Garbers said.

"I might get the vapors too," I said.

"Reed Two is supposed to be badder than Reed One," Garbers said. "It makes sense, doesn't it?"

"Dyer's only after the birds," DeGuerra said.

"I forgot," Garbers said.

"And that's it?" I asked. "You aren't looking any further into it?"

"Falling out among scumbags," DeGuerra said. "How much further do we have to look? We're already holding our noses."

"We'll find Lupe Jackson and get her for plugging Cady," Garbers said. "And if anything points to you, we'll talk again."

"Well, good luck." I got off the hot seat.

"Oh yeah," DeGuerra said. He turned off the tape recorder. "This is the part I like. Dyer, you been breaking every law known to man."

"And to me," Garbers said.

"And to her," DeGuerra said. "Leaving the scene of a crime, disturbing the scene of a crime, failure to report crime after crime."

"You forgot destruction of telephone company property."

"That, too," DeGuerra said. He told Garbers, "He ripped out Jackson's phone."

"What a miscreant," Garbers said.

"A sleuthing miscreant," I said.

74

"I'd lock you up for all this," DeGuerra said, "except then you probably wouldn't ask me out to your porch anymore to watch the sun sinking slowly over the Coyote Mountains."

"And to drink," I said.

"That too." DeGuerra cleared his throat. "In my official capacity I should tell you, you been cooperating in your own half-assed way. Next time you come across a dead guy, no matter how much he had it coming, hang around until we get there. Save us all a lot of hassle."

"You know where I live."

"Just do it," DeGuerra said. "Or we won't merely exercise our authority. We'll stick it to you. It'll be a lot more inconvenient for you than this little talk."

"The old lady, what's-her-name, Edwina Garrett. She backed you up," Garbers said. "So did Allison Crews. Otherwise we might not be so forgiving."

"Just how I thought of you."

DeGuerra poked me again. "How are you and Allison getting along? Hope you don't have your hands full with heisted birds."

The two of them laughed me out the door.

18

Sleep hurtled by with no time for dreams. Before dawn I was on the road again, hung over from the bashing I'd taken and feeling generally behind. I drove on autopilot east and south, out into the open country beneath the Santa Ritas, the range a silhouette against the coming sunrise. There was a dirt road climbing the *bajada* and I took it. The cactus thinned out and tall grasses stepped in. The grass was pale before the rains.

All of it was public land, but the public was absent, shuttered in the city in various cubicles. Rabbits, bruiser desert hares, grudgingly tiptoed to the sides of the road and watched me go by. Doves spooked out of the grass and wheeled off. A lone coyote, looking leaner than its reputation, crossed in front of me and disappeared in the brush. I had the urge to trade places with it.

Before I could, there was the black Corvette, city sleek and polished, like a gun or a fast woman, with the requisite blackened windows. Parked, locked, no one inside, not even a fast woman. I started walking up the road, the natural direction for creatures being pursued, and thus also for pursuers.

I read the land and used my ears. The light had filled in the long view of the city and the other ranges across the valley.

There wasn't any bird noise. The birds were hiding. The man from the Corvette had come this way.

Off to the right there was a rustling, a shout, and a flock of black birds lifted at once in tight formation. A falcon arose behind them and gave chase. It was a peregrine, gaining speed and altitude, closing fast on its scythelike wings. It cut into the flock, which parted magically to let it through and reformed behind it. Starlings from the looks of them. They maneuvered quickly as one, darting left, left again, then right, a rippling matador's cape of birds. The peregrine stalled above them, tucked its wings and launched a dive. They swept around; the peregrine corrected and slammed into them, closed its talons on nothing but air. The little birds had flicked twenty yards in the other direction. They were too quick for this particular peregrine. It climbed doggedly, dived into them again. The contest covered cubic acres of atmosphere, not much ground. I found the man underneath who was running it.

He was dressed like a prowler caught out at daybreak, in a black long-sleeved shirt and black trousers and a black beret. He had the falconer's glove sheathing his left arm and was wearing more leather, enough to be a hobby in itself: a wide belt slung with pouches and knee-high lace-up boots. Inside the trappings he was built soft around the middle and in the face, with mushroom skin and unbarbered black hair, mustache, and beard. A red patch on his beret advertised a rock and roll band. He was some age between twenty and forty, his face unlined and uncommitted. He stood in a grassy opening ringed by mesquite, neglecting me.

"Al Burabi," I said. He watched the bird-fight, which had drifted in the breeze.

"Get your shit together," he yelled. He had the Arabic accent, corrugating his words, as if he had phlegm.

The peregrine smacked into the flock and managed to knock down a single starling. The little bird fell limply into the tall grass. Burabi uttered something in Arabic.

"You'll lose it in there," he yelled.

The peregrine circled low over the grass, seeming hesitant,

confused. The surviving starlings had fled. Burabi walked toward the spot where the one had dropped.

"Come down," Burabi called. He gestured with his glove. The peregrine beat its way over, leather jesses trailing off its legs. I thought it might overshoot. It held up at the last second, stalled, and dropped lightly onto the glove.

Burabi secured the peregrine, snapping the jesses to a leash, snapping the leash to a ring on the glove. "Back with nothing," he said.

The peregrine stared at him without emotion. It had different shadings than the ones I was trying to recover. Its chest was sandy white, its back flat gray. The stare was impenetrable.

"You learn," Burabi told the peregrine. He bent over and separated the grass and picked up the dead starling by one wing. There was an incision along its flank, and blood. The bird was broken. Its iridescence was fading, that quickly.

"This is trash. A trash bird," Burabi said. He stuffed the starling into one of the pouches on his belt and closed the flap over it. The peregrine screamed at him.

Burabi looked at me for the first time. "A loud, complaining bird," he said. "And you?"

"Not so loud," I said.

Burabi smiled broadly. He had a cultured manner that went with his softness. He didn't seem threatened or surprised by my stalking him, and I wasn't the least threatening person. At least, I hoped I wasn't.

I tried to look even more unsavory, and springing off my last twenty-four hours, I must have had some success. Burabi took a step back.

"Who are you, and what's your business here?" he asked.

Men who dress in black shouldn't be taken straight on. I made up some things. "William Bonney. I'm interested in peregrines."

"So."

"I want one. I'll pay."

Burabi smiled again. His peregrine screamed.

"Not this one," I said. "You'll have to get somebody else to take him off your hands. I want a fresh one. A wild one."

"So you think of me?"

"You share my interest." Burabi waited. "You want a wild one for yourself," I said. "You've made inquiries."

"How do you know this? How do you find me?"

"We know some of the same people."

"Falconers? Are you a falconer?"

"Just getting into it. And I figure I'll start with the best. I'll deal with your supplier. Maybe we can get a volume discount—you can take a commission."

"They don't give discounts."

"So you have a supplier?"

"Possibly I was speaking in general terms."

Burabi was patient. But his peregrine was not. It did more of the screaming. Burabi winced, acting it out.

"Raise a bird in a cage," he said, "it grows up rude, with bad manners."

"People are the same way."

Burabi studied me. "Help us scare up breakfast," he said. He straightened his arm and uttered another command in his own language. The peregrine spread its wings, took off lazily, and began to climb in spirals.

Burabi watched the peregrine diminish above us. It became a tiny black cross against the sky.

"We wouldn't hunt like this in Saudi Arabia," he said. "This is the United States method, suitable for a captive-bred. It takes very small skill for the falcon, and for me also. A woman could do it. The advantage is all with us."

He had me walk twenty yards out through the grass. We crossed some ground like that, on a sweep. The peregrine had reached its pitch high overhead and was circling. Waiting on.

There were birds around us in the grass. They didn't want to fly. They knew the falcon was up there.

A covey of quail exploded under my feet. They had held out as long as possible. They flew a few yards and tucked back into the grass. The peregrine didn't respond. Burabi stomped around where the quail were lying up. They took off and went to ground again. When Burabi stomped after them he flushed something else that was also hiding. A mourning dove. It wasn't pudgy like the quail, it relied on speed to outrun any predator. It raced horizontally away from us with its white wing feathers flashing.

"Now you watch," Burabi said.

The peregrine folded and dropped. The mourning dove sensed it coming and changed course and the peregrine adjusted. There was more fine tuning between them. The peregrine was pure speed streaking down. At the last moment it threw its talons forward and then crashed into the dove. We could hear the impact clearly, despite the distance. Burabi grunted. Losing feathers, the dove tumbled down. The hit had killed it. The peregrine swooped up and around and down and grabbed the dove before it could finish its tumble into the tall grass. The peregrine carried it off, landed, spread its wings, and mantled possessively over the body. It began to pluck the dove and then tore into the flesh.

"He can eat a little," Burabi said.

We walked slowly toward the peregrine and its prey.

"You think this is cruel?" Burabi said.

"No more so than everything else."

"It is cruel," Burabi said. "And you're correct about everything else." He was pushing me for a reaction. "But what we do to birds is worse, because it has purpose. For many years in Europe there was a practice called seeling. To tame a wild hawk, its eyelids would be sewed shut."

We were within range of the raw sounds of eating. The peregrine guarded its kill and screamed at us. Burabi peeled a strip of raw beef out of one of his pouches. He offered the beef in his gloved fist while he worked his way in. He talked to the peregrine, persuaded it to hop onto the glove and rip into the beef. He grabbed what was left of the dove carcass and shoved it in the pouch where the dead starling had gone. The peregrine gulped down the beef strip and screamed for more.

"That's enough," Burabi told it. "I keep him hungry, so he

attends me," he said. "But strong so he can hunt. His natural weight minus ten percent is good. I starve him only a little."

Burabi preened his peregrine, cleaning twigs and bits of vegetation out of its feathers and tail. He took a plastic spray bottle out of a holster and sprayed water mist on the bird.

"To cool him down," he said. "I do so much for him."

"What's his name?"

Burabi spit in Arabic. "Roughly translated it means Doom, Death, and Destruction. Your language is so timid. As if it's meant to be spoken by old ladies." He displayed the peregrine on his glove. "Notice how the dark feathers around the eyes cut the glare. His beak is hooked for tearing flesh from bones and snapping necks. His shape offers no resistance to the wind. He is a top-of-the-line killer. His kind understands exactly what we want from them. So the price would be high."

"How high?"

Burabi looked at the mountains, the sun just lancing over them. "Peregrines are very much in demand in Saudi Arabia," he said. "They go from your desert to our desert and perform well. We were using their kind, the long-wings, to hunt for us since before your Jesus Christ came along. We didn't get into it for sport, we did it to catch food, and we were not so much concerned with melodrama. We don't hurl our peregrines into the sky like you do over here, we fly them straight after the quarry. Like I was trying with this one, only he doesn't get it. We ride out in great caravans, in trucks or on horseback, all the men with peregrines, and sometimes with dogs, the salukis. We speed along and flush our quarry and ride it down, and when we get close we launch our peregrines off the fist. Even so the outcome is always in doubt, because the peregrines do not have the advantage of altitude; they start even with what they hunt. It's something to see, and to do."

"Is this the sales pitch?"

"If you like. Are you looking for a male or a female?"

The question implied he had access to a pair.

"Either one."

"Myself, I prefer the males. They are smaller, yet more responsive. It's true generally, don't you think, that males are the better performers?"

"That depends."

"You talk like a lawyer. Is that what you are?"

"No. I'm a mechanic."

"You are not a mechanic," Burabi said. He stroked the peregrine. "This is his last hunt of the summer. Any day he will begin the molt. I gave him drugs to delay it."

"What's the problem?"

"The problem, Billy Bonney or whoever you are, is you. You pretend to be what you are not. You have hands made for punching and a face for that too."

"I can't change that."

"You try to trap me into something."

"I offer you a chance to make some money."

"That is something I care nothing about."

"Then why tease me?"

"I was curious. I have no peregrines for sale."

"Do you know of any?"

"No."

He was lying and he wanted me to know it. The lies may have been big or small. Mostly they were aloof. I could have shoved him around, but usually there are better, more effective ways to go about it, even with men in black.

"Call me if you reconsider," I said. I took out a business card and tucked it in his shirt pocket. He took it out.

"'Coyote Enterprises Unlimited'—what is this?"

"Call me and find out." Then I was temporarily out of strategy. I walked back to the Scout, copied down the license plate on his Corvette, and left.

Burabi wasn't much of a lead, or I wasn't much of a detective, or both, but I had to take what I could get. I stopped at a country store and called Lew Santiago. He did stakeouts and tail jobs for me. I gave him Burabi's name and car facts. "Get his address and stay on him."

"What am I looking for?" Lew asked.

"Birds."

"Yeah? What kind and how many?"

"Peregrine falcons. Two. Open your bird book and take a look. He's got another one of his own that doesn't count."

"Are these falcons stuffed or alive?"

"As you and me."

"That isn't saying much," Lew said. "You know what time it is?"

I told him it would be the usual rate.

19

Desierto Lindo, subdividerese for Pretty Desert, seemed like anything but. Much of the development was raw dirt, bladed level in preparation for the housing concept we all deserve. That was how the billboards had phrased it, pointing me deep into the foothills of the Tortolitas, offering visions of forever red sunsets over luxurious back patios and putting greens that stretched to the horizon, enjoyed by undissipated and un-lonely senior citizens, starting in the low six figures.

Half the golf course was in, lush and garishly green on the little graded hills. It looked like a cheap toupee on the desert, maintained by chugging sprinklers. Spaced around a nearby cul-de-sac were the model homes, the stately Saguaro and the elegant Cholla and the more affordable Prickly Pear. The town home cluster was titled Cactus Paradise.

The people behind it had gone with the desert motif. Native vegetation had been saved around the models and in strips along a meandering wash that served as the centerpiece. A cement walkway done in sandy brown had been laid along the bank and down to the bottom of the wash, to a little pool that must have been fed by a year-round spring. The golf course dog-legged around the upper rim of the pool, and the lower shore had been colonized by ramadas with concrete picnic tables and grills. It was a parody of what it had been, the water hole as the nucleus of desert life. In a field off to the north, dug-up trees from all over the development survived in formations, neat columns of mesquites and paloverdes with their roots boxed, waiting to be replanted in accordance with the master plan.

At least somebody had a plan; I was short. The sheriff's detectives were working the obvious: the known associates and hangouts of Reed Two and Lupe Jackson. Working the same was Game and Fish, in the person of Allison Crews. That merry-go-round was full. Left for me was the less obvious. Such as Desierto Lindo. Artie Jackson had tacked up a news clipping on the place before his throat got cut. Bruce Cady had done some consulting here before he got shot in the arm. I was going to find out what I could. My priorities were missing falcons, and keeping my body parts intact.

Flags waved on poles fronting the office, the dominant a colossal stars and stripes, the size they fly at the more patriotic auto lots and malls. Every year the flags seem to get bigger, as if there is more to prove, or discount, by their presence. There was also a standard Arizona flag, and the Mexican flag for crossover business, and another flag that was green, representing, I guessed, profits. Or ecology. Maybe the ecology of profits, or the profits of ecology. I should have known. It was the official Desierto Lindo flag, with the name spelled out in gold, and a gold saguaro.

I parked beside the office, in the rippling shadow of the big American flag, and stared off at the acreage that had been cleared. There was a lot of it. Birds hovered over the bare earth, fairly large birds searching for something they had lost. They were burrowing owls that had nested underground in rodent holes and started families. Then the graders had come through and sealed the burrows, burying the baby owls. The surviving adults were out looking. They would look a long time. It was a common sight that time of year all around the edges of the city.

A salesman with just the right smile pranced out of the office. He thought there was no way he wasn't slick.

"Pardner, you took the wrong turn," he said. He pointed to a trailer a quarter mile away that was hemmed in by pickups and heavy equipment. "Crew boss is over there. This is sales."

He was the type to have to see a card. I showed him one that made me a private investigator. He flustered. "What is this?"

The flag bothered me. It was overbearing, looming over us, snapping and rustling. "Let's go inside."

I got his name. It didn't matter. There were others like him posted among the cubbyholes and desks where they would run some numbers and do their closings, and they didn't matter either. The head man took me over. Everything about him mattered.

Sax Leonard. He had the hair, the looks, the clothes. Fiftyish and trim and armored by pleasantries. Eyes that gave it away. A handshake that was anything I wanted to make of it.

Effortlessly he cut me out of the pack and drew me into his private office, where he had potted cactus dying in the corners and furniture made out of well-oiled mesquite and tubular chrome. Mounted on a table was a replica of what Desierto Lindo would look like when the burrowing owls had moved on. Little plastic houses and town homes on streets that curved around the golf course and the washes and remnants of desert. A plastic clubhouse with a swimming pool and shuffleboard and tennis courts painted around it. Little plastic trees and plastic cactus, but no little plastic people. Their loan applications were pending.

"You're a private eye, eh? A shamus?" Leonard asked. "Interesting line of work. Have a seat." I did. The chair was too comfortable. If it hadn't been that, it would have been something else. Leonard remained standing. He was treating me like a prospect. "Something to drink?"

He had a wet bar along one wall, under posters for Desierto Lindo, which showed mostly desert and very little development. Around the margins were drawings of the wildlife that had been living there first. They had a nice one of a little owl, not the burrowing kind but the screech owl that lives in holes in the saguaros. NATURE FOR A NEIGHBOR was the slogan.

Leonard opened a half refrigerator under the bar. "Ginger ale? Coke? Beer?"

I had a ginger ale, Leonard the same.

"From the can okay?" he asked. He popped open the cans and put mine on a little leather coaster on the desk. I had a swig and looked at the coaster. Embossed on it was DESIERTO BELLO.

"We dropped that," Leonard said. "People didn't know how to pronounce it. Made them feel foolish. Last thing you want in this business."

"I'm here about Artie Jackson," I said.

"Artie Jackson. Is he some ballplayer?"

I let him alone. He had some ginger ale.

"Can't place him," he said.

"You had something in common. He was into animals."

"Great." Leonard had some more ginger ale. "Look, I'm being cordial with you. You know I don't have to be. I've got nothing to hide, nothing to be ashamed of, nothing to be embarrassed about, but I've got better things to do than stand around trying to psych out some worn-out PI."

"What happens when you're not this cordial?"

"Just make yourself clear."

It hadn't taken much to blow away his hospitality. Or had it? "Jackson was killed yesterday morning," I said. "It was in the news."

"I read the business section, and *The Wall Street Journal*. He wasn't mentioned."

"He should have been. He was an entrepreneur. He trapped and sold wildlife illegally."

"Hardly the kind of man I would have any association with."

"He'd been reading up about Desierto Lindo. He saved an

article about it, put it up on his bulletin board with exclamation points around it."

"That's your evidence?"

"I wouldn't put it that strongly." But Leonard had.

"There must be hundreds of people who've clipped out stories about this development," Leonard said. "Make that thousands. This is a quality place, a unique residential experience. Escape the city without giving up the city's amenities."

"I know the slogan."

"Correct. We're giving the public what they desire. The place might look a little rough now, but by the time we're done it'll be better than it was to begin with. You won't be able to tell we weren't always part of the landscape. We're emphasizing every single natural resource. We're retaining the native vegetation and all the ecology." He was a little clumsy with the jargon. "We conserve while we create. We'll have quail on the patios, squirrels on the roof, coyotes on the fairways. A generation will settle here. They've worked all their lives to make it to where they can move out and live in harmony on the land, and that's what we're offering. A second chance, a chance to live in peace and quiet with the plants and the animals and a tournament-level golf course. That's why so many write-ups have been done on this place, even though it'll be months before anyone moves in. They're lining up to buy, because they know a good thing."

"What's your position here?"

"My position? I'm president of the firm." He slipped a card from the deck cradled in lucite on his desk and handed it to me. "Sax Leonard, Inc. That's me."

"You put up the money for all this?"

"You are it, you really are," Leonard effused. "I don't mind telling you there's no one else but me and the banks. I'm the kit and kaboodle. I'm like that entrepreneur you're so interested in, only I didn't make it in skins."

"Got any other developments going?"

"That's a strange question."

88

He was a man with strong motives. I wondered where they aimed. "Is the answer strange?"

"Not at all. This is the only project I have going at the moment. I've been years building up to it."

"So it's important to you that this place succeed."

Leonard narrowed his eyes. "Very important. And it's going to. We seem to be straying off the subject of this guy who got his throat cut."

"I didn't say anything about his throat. I said he got killed."

"He's just some dead guy now. There's no tie-in with me or Desierto Lindo."

"Maybe Jackson was tied in with someone else who's working here. You've got a large staff."

"I'm sure he wasn't. This is a white-collar bunch."

"Then you won't mind if I ask around?"

"Of course I mind. We're here to sell houses, not to make ourselves available for interrogation. If you had anything more to go on, maybe I'd say yes. I'm as interested in solving crimes as the next guy. But you don't have anything. So stay away from the staff, unless you're a customer."

"Maybe I'm thinking of buying in."

"Prices are low this early. Someone would be happy to explain the terms."

"Not just yet. First I have other things to go on."

"Like what?"

"Bruce Cady."

"What's he got to do with this?"

"You know him, then?"

"Bruce did a job for me. For the development. Don't tell me—is he dead too?"

"No. He's been shot, though. Something else in the news."

"Maybe I did see something on that. How'd it happen again? Some gal?"

"Jackson's widow did it."

"Now I see what you're getting at, now I'm reading you. It can't be related to Bruce's work here. He hasn't been around for months. He turned in his report the end of last summer."

"It was a biological survey of the property?"

"Correct. He filled in for the county; I guess they were too busy down there. Done all the time."

"What did his report show?"

"The usual stuff."

"Usual how?"

"I don't have the details in front of me. He came out and hiked all over the place and gave us a list of the plants and animals that are out here. Made some recommendations, none of which were binding, but most of which we're following anyway. You see what we're doing with the trees?"

"Yeah."

"Bruce didn't find anything that would hold us up. His recommendations had no force of law behind them."

"I'd like to see his report."

"There's a copy around here somewhere. Come back in a couple of days and I'll have it located."

"Artie Jackson do any work for Cady?"

"Stop it with Jackson. I told you, he's zip as far as I'm concerned. I never heard of him, so how can I say if he knows Bruce Cady?"

"Knew. He's dead."

"So it goes."

20

Leonard wouldn't let me leave without a couple of the brochures for Desierto Lindo. "If you don't want them, just leave them around," he said. "It won't hurt."

He hustled me through the office to ensure I'd have no further contact with the sales force. He needn't have bothered. I had been sized up and branded a looky-loo, a waste of time compared to the oldsters who were wandering into the maw.

Outside, the flags were still rippling in a breeze that was doing little else. The sun had taken over the morning. I singed myself on the front seat of the Scout and started out the long driveway. Something coming in behind a Buick diverted my attention from the heat waves.

It was a yellow VW sand buggy, with a woman at the wheel. A brown woman with a mane of black hair. I slowed and watched Lupe Jackson go past and recede in my rearview. She hadn't noticed me, or didn't care. She beat the Buick to a parking spot under the flags, brushed off a salesman, and marched into the office.

I found a good spot to watch without being seen. Twenty minutes later Lupe Jackson left the office and drove toward the highway and me. She turned north, and I kept her company from a discreet distance. I looked for a place to do it.

She helped me by turning off on a dirt road. A lot of

Arizona has changed for the worse, but most of our roads are still dirt. This one moseyed into open desert with straight stretches and easy curves. I nudged the gas and came up behind her buggy and pulled out as if to pass. There was a lot of dust behind us and no one around to see. We were going about thirty-five. She figured it out and tried to speed ahead, but her buggy wasn't up to it. I swerved and banged her off the road. The buggy was a lightweight against the burly old Scout. She crashed it into the brush and hung up on some rocks, and when she got out to run I had to tackle her. She was busy with those boots, kicking me. I sat on her legs, and that didn't do it either. She twisted and grabbed into her purse and came out with her zip gun, and I slapped it away. Then she had a folding knife that she flicked open one-handed. I got a forearm in the way and latched on to her wrist and took possession of the knife. She pretended to give up. Then she started slugging me and I had to hit her, openhanded but sincerely. She cursed me and relaxed.

"You like to hit women," she said.

"Ones I'm sitting on. It's only safe that way."

She breathed under me while I held the knife out of her reach. She had loosened the spring and oiled it. I flicked it open and closed a few times and complimented her work.

"Give it to me. I'll show you what it's meant for."

I said no thanks and threw the knife somewhere. I snagged her purse and pawed through it. Nothing new. But she did have the little jar from her refrigerator, with the pickled frog inside.

"It has sentimental value," she said.

I looked at the frog.

"Cute, huh?" she said.

I put the jar down and tossed her purse away. "Leonard told me he was paying you off," I said. "Where is it?" Instead of issuing denials she renewed her struggles. I burned up some calories rolling her over and pinned her on her stomach so she couldn't get at me, frisked her pockets and didn't have such a bad time doing it. She was a lot of lively woman. I could feel guilty about all this later. In a back pocket of her shorts was a roll of new cash: hundreds, one after the other, adding up to three thousand. I stood up with the money. She got right-side up and tried to light me on fire with her eyes.

"What is this?" she demanded. "You robbing me?"

"Not of anything that belongs to you."

"That money is mine."

"Where'd you get it?"

"I had it buried out back of the hut."

"No you didn't. The stuff you dug up had been around. This is virgin."

"How would you know?"

"I get around too."

She got up, rubbing herself here and there. Both of us were dusty and stuck with fragments of plants.

"You working for Leonard now?" she asked. "You work for anybody that comes along?"

"Anybody with cash."

"Then keep some of that and work for me too. You can start by going back and beating the shit out of Leonard."

"What for?"

"For going back on our deal. For sending you after me."

"He just wants his money back, that's all."

"Well, fuck him. He got off cheap."

"He doesn't think so."

"You don't work for Leonard. You don't know shit."

"I know where three thousand bucks is."

"It's legit. Leonard owed me for a job: Artie did some collecting out on his land. Some snakes and stuff, I think a Gila monster or two. Things that might bite the rich assholes moving in there. Leonard wanted it safe."

I picked up the pickled frog. "Did Artie collect this?"

"I don't know where he got it. It's just a frog, man."

"What happened to the haul from Desierto Lindo?"

"What d'you think, he wanted rattlers for pets? He sold them. He only got a couple hundred on that end. The big thing was that Leonard wanted his place cleaned out."

"Why'd Leonard pay in cash? Why not a check?"

"I prefer cash," she said, and it was the one thing that was entirely true. "If you're not working for Leonard you better give me that money back."

"Why? You going to report me to the cops?"

"I will."

"Go ahead. We'll go in together. I'd like to hear you explain why you shot a guy yesterday and how your husband just happened to get dead."

"You know I didn't kill Artie."

"Maybe. But you did the shooting."

"Cady had it coming," she said.

"Why's that?"

"He's a white man, isn't he?" She wouldn't elaborate.

"Cady says you were trying to sell him the falcons."

"That would have been a trick. I told you, I didn't even have them."

"Where are they?"

"What about that?" She pointed to the cash.

"You help me, you keep it."

"It's mine already."

I shrugged. "You know how white men are."

"What about the cops?"

"They can do their own thing."

"Okay. You hand over the money first."

I did. She fingered the bills and refolded them into her pocket. "Reed Two has the birds."

"Did he kill Artie?"

"You'll have to ask him—better watch yourself when you do. He won't like it that you offed his brother."

"I had help."

"You'll need it this time too. I'll tell you something. Reed Two is a lot tougher than Reed One. Reed Two can fight. He beat a bobcat to death once when it clawed him. That's how he got his face. He had the cat trapped and thought it was dead, only it wasn't. A bobcat will do that, lie still and wait.

They don't fight the trap like other animals do. They just wait for their chance for payback."

Her looks had gotten more primitive. She saw a chance for some payback of her own, against Reed Two, maybe against me.

"He's got the birds out at his camp. I'll tell you where."

"You'll take me there."

Reluctantly, she agreed. "Man, this hero act, it's strictly out of the fifties. You get here in a time machine? You drive that Scout, you dress like this." She waved at my shirt, a loose thing made to never be tucked in, with two chest and two belly pockets. L. L. Bean's best.

"I like this shirt," I told her.

"It's you," she said.

Before we could get into stripes versus plaids and where the hankies should be tucked, I collected her zip gun and the little jar with the pickled frog, slipped them into my belly pockets. She got her purse, and for public relations I let her keep the knife. I made her ride with me in the Scout, which technically was out of the early sixties. I didn't want to have to run her into the ditch again.

21

She was in a hurry. "Can't this thing go any faster?" She slapped the split vinyl on the dash. "What do you have this old beater for anyway?"

"It goes fast enough for me."

"Not for me. I want to get this done."

"Reed Two on his way somewhere?"

She slapped the dash again. "The deal we got doesn't include all this stuff. Just I show you the falcons for the three thousand."

"What kind of deal do you have going with him?"

"I make lots of deals."

"Good ones?"

"Good, bad. I'm not going to say any more."

"You scared?"

"I sure am. You should be too. If you aren't, you're stupid."

I was feeling pretty smart, which meant she was probably right. She kept us going on the dirt road, which got us way out on the far side of the Tortolitas. We hit the old two-lane to Phoenix, all but abandoned after the interstate went in twenty miles south. The only sign of civilization—and that was debatable—was a patch of trailers and shanties where a biker gang from out of state had set up a relay for drugs and underage women. Nobody bothered to catch them at it. It was that kind of country.

Some miles beyond the bikers she had me turn off the paved road onto an unmarked track leading more or less north. It got rougher. I dropped into four-wheel. She was cursing.

"My buggy'll take the bumps better than this," she said. "Don't slow down. We got a ways to go."

Mesquite and ocotillo and cactus scratched their fingernails along the sides of the Scout. We just fit through. "Let's go, let's go," she said.

"You act like somebody's after us."

That seemed to calm her down. "No," she said. "Just the loco ahead. I don't think you can take him. I don't want to walk out of here with him after me for doing this."

We bounced around. She had the muscles in her arms and legs and didn't jiggle much.

"Stop here," she said. "Pull in there." The track ended. There was a wide spot before the brush closed in. No other vehicles. She slid over and pinched the inside of my thigh.

"I saw you looking," she said. "You like my body?"

She moved her hand around. I tried to pry it off me. She grabbed harder.

"I didn't come out here for this," I said.

"Yes you did. You admit you're a white man. You want a Mexican lover."

"I told you. Falcons."

"They're here. Just up the wash a little ways. You can fool with me a little bit and then go and get them."

I extricated myself out from under her hand, and out of the Scout. "We go together. For all I know nothing's up there. Or more than you say."

"He's up there," she said. "He's expecting me. But I wasn't going to come back. I was through with him."

"Your mind changes like the breeze."

"We didn't get it on, if that's what you're wondering," she said. "He'd be the last guy."

"What am I? The second-to-last?"

She saw I wasn't going for her. It made her in a hurry again. "He'll be mad. I'll take you near and that's it." She brushed between some paloverdes and jumped down into the wash that was right there. It was wide, maybe thirty yards across, with eroded banks that were guarded by thickets of low trees. The middle of the wash was clear, a bed of gravel and sand and half-buried tree limbs that had been washed down in floods. It was dry when we saw it.

We walked up the wash, Lupe Jackson in the lead, me watching her and the banks and the way ahead. Mostly I watched her. I had my gun out, the .38 with the four-inch barrel. It was not the right gun for all this open space, but I hadn't had time to pack. We should have been up on the banks, where there was cover, but that way would have been thorny and slower, and she had wanted us to go this way. She was putting a lot of oomph into her walk. She was some distraction; either she was always like this or she had a reason.

We sweated our way up. The sun had stalled directly overhead and there was no shade where we were. I began to wish for the canteen in the Scout. Around two bends she angled toward the right bank and leaned against it. "Around there," she said. The wash curved again and I couldn't see past. She moved slowly ahead along the bank, being careful where she stepped. We got an angle and then we could see the camp.

It wasn't much, just a couple of logs around a rock fire ring, and a lean-to of branches propped against the bank. In the rainy season it would have all washed out. A pickup was parked beyond the lean-to in the shade of some overhanging trees, a Ford, plenty worse for wear, no plates. Hanging from limbs over and around it were coyotes, just heads and skins, strung one inside the other on ropes, layers and layers of dead coyotes. He must have had fifty of them. And there were rabbits, bobcats, other things that had been alive. And a stink and flies buzzing, which we couldn't miss even from where we were. He had been tossing the guts and parts wherever. He wasn't in view.

Lupe Jackson pointed to the pickup and whispered, "Falcons."

He had them in the shade. He knew that much. I could see the top of the plywood and chicken wire cage in the pickup's bed.

She whispered, "*Buena suerte*," and tried to slip past me, back the way we had come. I held on to her arm.

He could have been circling behind us, sighting in on us with anything from a sniper rifle to a bow and arrow. What he was doing was a little less couth.

There was thrashing on the far bank by the lean-to, and a man and a half appeared in torn bib overalls, boots, and no shirt. His jumbo hands were out of scale for the button fly on his overalls, but he got it undone, and he stood up there on the bank and took a leak. His stream arced out and down into a rusty tin can on the floor of the wash. He got most of it into the can. It was artful, as such things go.

Reed Two buttoned himself up, jumped down, and strode past the can without looking at it. There was a canvas sack roped over his shoulder, and when he got near the pickup he threw it off, opened it, and pulled out more dead things: another coyote, a fox, some others; fresh skins that were bloody and limp. He turned on a boom-box radio that was lodged in the fork of a mesquite and music pounded out, sounding so totally bad it had to be punk rock. So he was a punk redneck.

Lupe Jackson tried to pull away from me again, and I shoved her against the bank, starting a little avalanche of dirt and stones. We listened to the punk rock while Reed Two worked on the skins. I tapped the barrel of my pistol against her boots and made her understand I wanted them off. I got her socks too, tucked them in the boots and threw the boots in the tangle up on the bank where it would take her some time to find them. I'd spent much of the day throwing her things around. But if she was going to run, it would hinder her.

I had ideas about how to take the big man, all of them risky. I could climb the bank and work my way closer through the brush, but he might sense it, even over the punk rock; it was his turf. Or I could walk up the wash in the open and act friendly. He didn't look like a man with any friends. He must have had guns, though I couldn't see any. I made a decision.

I got a clean view exposing little of myself and used two hands to cock and aim the pistol. Lupe Jackson thought I was going to blow him away. She didn't mind. The distance was about fifty yards, not an easy shot but one I should make or get out of the business. Call it my version of pissing in a can.

I banged at the radio that was making all the noise. It spun out of the tree and the punk rock was no more. Reed Two stood up and I bracketed him with two more in the dirt.

"Face down," I yelled in my best authoritative voice.

He looked at what he could see of me.

"The radio was a lot smaller than you are," I yelled.

He lay down. With his size, it took some time.

It was as simple as that.

22

I had Lupe Jackson front me going in. She picked her way on
bare feet, cursing me. She'd been doing a lot of that. The big
man was less upset. He lay there complacently watching our
approach, realizing that his opposition amounted to, at most,
the two of us. I flicked open the cylinder on the .38 and
inserted three good cartridges where the spent ones were. He
was gauging me.

"You wrecked my tunes," he said. "My loony tunes."

The conversation had possibilities, but instead I looked
around for his guns. There was a .44 Magnum in a western
holster hung on a tree and a .30-06 hunting rifle in the lean-to.
And a nasty sawed-off twelve-gauge under the seat of the
truck. I rounded up all of them, and then I had a thought.

"Let's have the fare-thee-well," I told him.

"Make yourself happy," he said. He reached under himself
and tossed it my way: a double-barreled .45 derringer, just the
two shots, a hole blower from arm's length and useless at twice
that distance.

"So you bring him right on in," he said to Lupe Jackson.

She was keeping away from him. "He made me," she said.
"See, he took my boots. I thought you could handle him."

"I can," he said.

The falcons were indeed in the pickup. They were

lethargic. They'd been hooded and boxed for more than a day, unless he'd given them a break. I got a canteen and flicked water over them.

"Hey," he said. "I'm getting up."

"Go ahead. You'll make a better target."

"Oh please don't shoot me," he said, pitching his voice high like a frightened woman or kid.

He stood up and up and up. He must have been six foot five. And wide. I'd only seen Reed One after dark, but it wasn't just good lighting that made Reed Two look more formidable. He had his dirty red hair pulled left and right into two pigtails sticking down past his bare shoulders, banded in a rainbow of rubber bands. The old scars inflicted by the bobcat made a web on the lower quarter of his face. Between the scars and on the other three quarters, he had red freckles so close together he seemed sunburned. Eyebrows so pale they could have been illusions. Hard blue eyes. Clean-shaven, except that makes it sound all right. Crooked nose, lipless mouth, bad teeth. One earring, a dangling silver cross. Below all that, a continuation of the dense freckles, and denser muscles.

"What are you hassling me for?" Looking down at me.

"Let's see," I said. "There's so many things." I gestured around the camp, ending with the falcons. "And, oh yes, murdering Artie Jackson."

"You're not the cops."

"No, but I better bring you in as an offering."

He asked Lupe Jackson, "Who is this guy?"

"Some detective. He wasted your brother."

"He couldn't have."

"He says he had help," she said.

"If I have to, I'll put a bullet in your leg," I told him. He was making me skittish.

"Oh please please don't," he said again in his other, freaky voice.

"I'll be going now," Lupe Jackson said.

"Stick around," I told her.

"I didn't hurt Jackson," he said. "We were pards."

"Jackson had the falcons," I said. "Then he was dead and the falcons were gone. You've got them now."

"I remember you," he said. "At Jackson's hut. You were the guy out in the yard. I saw you snoozing, then I come upon Jackson leaking blood inside. I couldn't do anything about that. I took the birds, yeah, but I didn't start him leaking. You must've seen who done it."

"I didn't."

"That's how it came down, man." As if for reassurance, or protection, he reached into his overalls for his smoked granny-style sunglasses, wired them over his eyes. The little black circles made bottomless holes on his face.

"If you didn't cut Jackson, who did?"

Reed Two looked at Lupe Jackson again. "How do I know? Maybe she did. Nine times out of ten it's the wife."

"Maybe it was the both of you."

"We don't get along that good."

"She isn't a pard too?"

"I thought she was. I sort of inherited her."

Lupe Jackson snorted and told both of us, "Quit fucking around."

I asked the big man, "Why take the falcons from Jackson?"

"He's got a use for them now? What's it to you anyway? You got something special for these birds?"

"That's all I'm in this for."

"Hell," he said. "You waste my brother for that?"

"You've got it wrong. It was him who looked me up."

"Just a couple of damn birds."

"I thought you had a buyer."

"She told you that? I just might."

"Who?"

"You want in? I don't talk into guns. Put it away and we'll see."

"No thanks. How'd all you pards locate these falcons to begin with?"

"Some clown. He was out clowning around and he saw them up there on the cliffs."

"Bruce Cady?"

Lupe Jackson answered first. "That's ridiculous" she said. Reed Two said nothing.

"Why'd you go see Cady yesterday?" I asked her.

"I picked his name out of the phone book. I was lonely."

"She gets that way," said Reed Two. "Hubby Artie had been dead, what, an hour already?"

On impulse I threw a lie at her. "Where's the thousand bucks Cady gave you?"

"What?"

"The thousand. Where is it?" I was trying to jolt her, run them into each other. The cash she'd just gotten from Sax Leonard smelled of blackmail—cheap blackmail, the kind they would think of—and if the two of them had squeezed Leonard they might have also tried Cady, for reasons I didn't know.

Reed Two watched Lupe Jackson while she figured out how to answer me. "Cady didn't give me anything," she said.

"Come on. I saw you count it."

"Bullshit." She told Reed Two, "He's bullshitting you."

"It's not me he's talking to," Reed Two said.

"He paid her all right," I said. "Didn't she mention it?"

"No," Reed Two said.

"There was nothing to mention," she said. "That cheap bastard said he was broke."

"How much did you get from Leonard?" Reed Two asked.

She looked at me, then at Reed Two. "Three thousand."

"That's a little more than we figured," he said. "You asked him for more? Is that all I should know about?"

"All I can tell you," she said. "Listen," she said to me. "I got to go. I got things to do."

"What's your hurry?" Reed Two asked her.

"I haven't done anything wrong," she told me.

"Not in the last thirty seconds or so," I said.

"I could meet you later," she said. "I will, honestly."

Reed Two laughed.

"This is fine right here," I said.

"The thing is," she said, "some people might be stopping through."

"What people?" Reed Two asked.

"Just some guys. Like maybe they're out hunting and they just stop in." She looked at me for help. The big man was moving toward her. I had to bring the .38 to his attention again. It had lost much of its effect.

"You ought to be watching her," he said. "She's the trickster."

"Shoot him in the leg," she yelled. "You said you were going to shoot him in the leg. He probably did kill Artie."

"It simply ain't true," Reed Two said. "Look at me. You can tell I'm giving it to you straight."

I looked at him. He looked like a scumbag.

Our talk was interrupted by two men, strangers with shotguns of their own, hiking around the bend and up to the wash toward us.

"Shit," Lupe Jackson said. "Where the hell are my boots?"

23

One of them was a happy Hispanic, overfed and underdressed in a gray tank top, red nylon shorts, and running shoes. The other one was Anglo, boyish and blond, with sideburns and an expression of practiced toughness. He wore jeans and cowboy boots and a short-sleeved cowboy shirt undone at the top to show the hair on his chest. Both of them wore drugstore sunglasses. They were laboring with the pump shotguns over their shoulders, sweating more than they had to. They were city.

"No way we want to meet these guys," Lupe Jackson said.

"Let's," I said.

They stopped ten feet away. "Blow," Sideburns said to me.

"No offense," said the happy one. "We have negotiations to conduct." He nodded at Lupe Jackson and Reed Two.

"I got nothing to negotiate with you," Reed Two said.

"You want him," Lupe Jackson said. "Not me."

"You must be," Sideburns said, drawling it out, "Lupe."

"Here," she said. "Take the money back to Leonard, we'll call it square." She held out the three thousand in hundreds.

"Who's Leonard?" Sideburns asked.

The happy one chuckled.

Sideburns looked at Reed Two. "She snitched you off, man."

"I don't care anymore," Lupe Jackson said. "Here, take the money." She stepped forward and tried to force the cash into the happy one's free hand. He let the hundreds fall into the sand, where they were scattered by a little wind. Lupe Jackson scrambled after the hundreds and that broke us all loose. Sideburns went after her, I went after the happy one, and Reed Two pivoted and kicked me down. I've been shot with less of an impact. He kicked me again and I lost the .38. I couldn't take in any air. Reed Two was cracking the happy one with whirling kicks. Sideburns fired the shotgun to get his attention but that was a bad idea. Reed Two swiveled and snatched it just like that and hurled it away. Sideburns tried a few punches that got blocked and then Reed Two let one through and took hold of the arm and straightened it like he was going to break it, but instead he bit down on the hand and Sideburns screamed and Reed Two bit off a finger and spit it into the sand.

"Pain pain pain," Reed Two yelled.

Sideburns was writhing in the sand, screaming. The happy one was down too. Reed Two surveyed the scene through his bottomless smoked sunglasses. He turned them on me.

"Oh please please don't hurt me," he said again in his freaky voice. "Is that what my brother said?" he asked.

Falcons or not, I got up and ran. He was after me. I got over to the bank and went up it with him whispering at my heels. He managed to trip me but he lost footing and slid down the bank and I got up and tore through bushes and trees that cut me. He thrashed behind me, too close and getting closer. I wasn't going to outrun him; he was going to take me apart, finger by finger. I ran into a stand of cholla cactus, the wicked kind that is skinny and tall with branches and the worst needles. I kicked one over and grabbed it at the base and uprooted it, driving the needles into my hands. He was right there. I turned on him and swung the whole cactus, five feet of it, a cactus bat. The cactus thudded into him and stuck. He veered off, did some screaming himself. The cactus broke apart with pods clinging to his arm, his shoulder, his head, thatches of the yellow needles sticking deep into him. A shotgun fired from the wash. The pickup started. I ran that way for a change.

Lupe Jackson had the pickup zigzagging down the wash. The happy one blasted in her direction with his shotgun. He got a window and some body panels. She drove around the bend and out of range. She had the falcons.

The happy one stood over Sideburns and turned his shotgun on the world. He shot in my direction, and at the bank on the other side. He reloaded and shot up the lean-to and the coyote skins. He wasn't as happy as he had been.

Finally he got tired of it and walked Sideburns down the wash in the direction everybody seemed to be headed. Sideburns had stopped screaming. His expression had changed to one of tight control. He hunched over his bloody hand. They took his chewed-off finger with them, wrapped in a rag, and stopped now and then for some of the hundreds that were blowing around.

Reed Two made wounded noises in the cactus patch. After a while I heard him moving downwash too.

24

I found my pistol, for all the good it would do me. I couldn't close my hands around it. They were lined solid with the cholla needles in the palms and swelling up, mostly numb, but starting to throb and make me a little dizzy. I did what I could without them: kicked through the fragments of the camp looking for clues to something other than my own shortcomings. The heat came back to bother me, and the flies with their buzzing.

I had let the situation get away from me. For the second time, I had lost the falcons.

I had a drink from a canteen. I had to use the heels of my hands to undo the cap, and I clamped the canteen between my forearms to tilt it to my mouth. The water helped. It did that for everyone in the desert, even me.

I found a pair of pliers and tried to use them to yank the cactus needles out of my hands. The needles had tiny hooks on the business ends that made them difficult. With the pliers and my teeth I plucked out some of the easiest ones. The hands were bleeding and no longer numb. Good thing nobody was around to watch. Then even that went bad.

I was listening for Reed Two or the others doubling back or I might have missed it: careful steps on the gravelly bed of the wash, coming closer. With two fingertips I holstered my little gun and took the pliers into hiding, up on the bank, where I'd been spending a lot of time.

A uniform stalked into view. Game and Fish issue. Filled out by Allison Crews. She had her pistol ready, sweeping the wash. I watched how she'd handle it, what she'd do. She saw how things had been kicked around, the lean-to shot up, the spent shotgun shells littering the sand. She picked up a shell and felt its warmth and dropped it. She tried to read tracks here and there. She thought it out. She holstered her gun and poked in the ruins of the lean-to, and where some gear was strewn around the fire ring. From the way she went about it, she was searching for something specific.

She grew disgusted and more abrupt. She dumped out a pack that she'd pulled out of the lean-to. She bent over the contents and picked up something like a tiny bracelet and put it in her pocket. I came out of hiding to find out what it was.

She pulled her gun again and held it on me, out of surprise—I hoped. "Henry. What brings you out here?"

"Working the falcons. What about you?"

"Same thing," she said. Some of her hair had come unpinned, giving her a less than official look. When I kept silent, she went on, "I've been asking around. I got word Reed Two uses this wash as one of his camps."

"He does."

"You ran into him? There was a fight."

"Sort of." I told her some of it.

"He bit off the guy's finger?"

"And spit it out."

"You expected him to eat it?" she said.

"Maybe he'd already had lunch."

"These shooters, what did they want?"

"They didn't make it clear. You got any ideas?"

"No. Why would I? How about you?"

"I know who to ask, and I'm going to enjoy it."

"You feel like sharing this information with me?"

"Sax Leonard."

"The developer? Why would he be mixed up in this?"

"He gave Lupe Jackson three thousand in cash this morning—why, I don't know, but I think she was double-crossing Reed Two as part of it—and I think Leonard decided to pull his own double-cross on both of them. She claimed the payment was for collecting snakes and other undesirables off Desierto Lindo."

"You asked me about Desierto Lindo yesterday. About Bruce consulting out there."

"You want to add anything?"

"You think I held out on you? What could there be to add?"

"Artie and Lupe Jackson, Reed Two—just about everybody in this case is tied to Desierto Lindo. Including Bruce Cady."

"If you want to define the case like that."

"How do you define it?"

"Differently. The Jacksons trapped the falcons, and then the Reeds moved on them."

"That doesn't explain all of it. Reed Two claimed he didn't kill Jackson, and he wasn't totally unconvincing. I think he and Lupe were blackmailing Leonard—before the double-crosses—and may have tried the same thing on Cady."

"That's absurd. What would they have on Bruce? Or Leonard, for that matter?" She tensed around her pistol, poked the barrel in my gut. "You've been trying to get something on Bruce all along. It doesn't sound like you've made it yet."

That made me angry. I said, "I was about to search the place when you showed up."

She changed the subject. "What happened to your hands?"

"I got into some cactus."

"I guess." She holstered her pistol. She took my hands and inspected them. "All these needles. You've got a forest of them here. What did you do, shake hands with a cholla?"

"Yeah."

"Trying to get away from Reed Two?" She took the pliers and began to tug out the needles. "This hurt?"

"No."

I let her work. After a while I said, "No use in me searching anyway. You already found what there was to be found."

She tugged out more needles, some of then breaking off. "You picked it up right there," I said. I stepped clear of her, over to where she'd dumped the pack, and shuffled through the jumble in the dirt. "What was it?" She stared at me while I toed around and exposed a bit of color. I picked it up, dropped it, picked it up again. There were still plenty of needles in my hands. It was a thin metal band, meant to be crimped around the leg of a captive bird of prey. The government issues them: every captive bird is assigned a number that is stamped on its leg band. In the way of governments, birds without numbers are illegal.

"You'll probably want this one too, for your . . . 'investigation.'"

She stared at me.

"It doesn't look counterfeit," I said. "It had to come from the feds, or maybe someone in Game and Fish, someone in government working with wildlife. We can probably find out who. They keep pretty close track of these."

"It came from me," she said. She took the leg band and tucked it in her pocket with the other one. "If you don't know already." She shook her head against a thought.

"I gave the leg bands to Reed—to the Reeds," she said. "I was working them on my own, before you even got involved. Undercover, on my own time, pretending to be another trafficker. I told them I had connections and got them the leg bands to prove it. They wanted to band birds they had taken, launder them and make them easier to sell. It made me sick. I thought I could put away the Reeds and get to the people they deal with. I busted my butt and now it's gone to hell."

"Describe Reed Two to me," I said.

"You've seen him."

"I'm waiting."

"He's big like his brother, with scars on his face."

"What part of his face?"

She told me the wrong side. "You never met Reed Two," I said. "The scars are over here. Who'd you really give the leg bands to? Cady? He told you about this camp. It's him, not you, who's been doing business with the Reeds. You're just taking the heat for him."

"This is pure fantasy," she said.

"That's why you had to shoot Reed One out at the cliffs—not once, but three times; to make sure he was dead, so he couldn't talk. You had the Magnum and one hit would have downed even him. But you had to keep him quiet about his dealings with your fiancé. You came out here today to suppress evidence, and maybe to kill Reed Two, so he couldn't talk either. Well? Doesn't that about sum it up?"

She burst out laughing. "Is this how you do it, Henry? I confess now? I would, but I don't have anything on my conscience."

I wished I could say the same.

25

My hands started hurting bad enough to send me hiking out. She came along. The sun didn't seem as hot, so I knew I was losing it. I made it to her Game and Fish pickup, the replacement she'd been issued, parked down a few bends of the wash. "You can't drive," she said. "Trust me that much?"

"Sure."

She had to work the door of the pickup for me. She drove us out to the highway and toward my place and finally gave me something to think about other than my hands.

"I was up all night on the shooting," she said. "Didn't even change clothes. Then I had an argument with Bruce this morning—the ceremony's on for tomorrow and I'm running around on this mess. So I got mixed up on Reed Two's scars. Does that convict me?"

"Anybody else know about this undercover you were doing?"

"No. I don't tell the department everything. You never did. Not until there are results. I can't believe you suspect me. You're just trying to write me off however you can."

"Forget it."

I needed a painkiller. I needed something to sterilize the holes in my hands. I needed whiskey. That was an old one, but true. I closed my eyes and the sun beat on them. Then we were pulling into the rocky driveway at my place, stopping in the shade of the overhanging mesquites by the house. I got out of the pickup before she could help me and had a joust with the house keys and the lock on the front door. I dropped the keys.

She said, "Let me do it."

I did it myself, making the needles worse. I went in and on through to the little courtyard that was my refuge—only a room where the roof had fallen in long ago, leaving bare adobe walls open to the sky and the canopy of mesquites, and what I'd left out there: a couple of old church pews facing a gutted TV cabinet, and my workbench and the shelf that held liquor. I dropped the bourbon bottle trying to lower it from the shelf. She picked up the bottle and slammed it on the workbench. The pew she jerked closer screeched on the eroded Mexican tiles.

"Stop it and sit down, Henry."

The walls closed in on me. I looked at the bourbon in its bottle. On the label was a handprint of my blood.

I sat. She got a bowl and poured whiskey in it and I dipped in my hands. The pain was therapeutic. She held the bottle to my lips and I had as much of that little charity as I could take. She got a pair of needle-nose pliers, appropriately named, and went to war on the cactus needles. She used tweezers and a knife. I gave her directions about the hooks on the ends of the needles. I was so amazingly competent. I was so full of crap.

"What's that smell?" she said. "Like formaldehyde. It's coming from your shirt, where it's soaked." She reached into my belly pockets for the things I'd taken off Lupe Jackson, before the fight. "There's a broken jar. And this? A frog?"

"It's a clue."

"Don't start hallucinating on me."

"Is there a zip gun too?"

"No. It must have fallen out." She hesitated. "You've got cuts from the glass and you're bleeding. The shirt's got to go."

She stripped the shirt off me, tended the cuts and buttoned

me into a fresh one. Her handling me like that stirred memories. She went back to work on my hands.

"You always hurt yourself somehow," she said. "That raft trip down the Gila? You just about lost an ear to the paloverde limb, and a big toe to those roots, and you had giardia for a month afterward."

"Yeah, and you got sunburned."

"I got a little red."

"And you took it out on those kids and their radio."

"They were polluting the whole canyon with that noise. You should talk. Didn't you just blow away Reed Two's boom box?"

"It made me think of you."

"That's easy. You ever try flipping one of those rafts?"

"The way you jumped onto theirs, they must have thought it was a pirate attack."

"They weren't kids. One was as big as you."

"You always liked a challenge."

"I still do," she said.

We thought about that, sitting side by side and staring at the blank glass face of the TV, the monumental husk of a floor model from the fifties, which I kept in front of the pews as a reminder of how not to spend my life. Out of nowhere, she said, "I miss coming out here."

I couldn't say anything to that and she didn't go on. Any lingering implications she avoided by leaving me again, but only to go for gauze and a higher-proof disinfectant from the crossroads store.

I looked at my hands. They were the hands I deserved. Maybe I'd find the falcons again. It would give me a chance to lose them again. I could set a record for finding falcons and losing them. They hadn't looked good in that box in Reed Two's pickup.

I went into the kitchen and forced my hands to pick up the phone, an old black model with a rotary dial. I was holding out on push buttons, extensions in every room, and call waiting. Laboriously I dialed the sheriff's detectives and asked for Sixto DeGuerra. I gave him the description of the pickup, now being driven by Lupe Jackson, loaded with contraband falcons.

"Plates?"

"Didn't have any when I saw it."

"Great." DeGuerra hung up. At least he'd shut off his laughing.

I tried another call, to Lew Santiago, who was tailing the Arab falconer, Al Burabi.

"Lew," Lew answered. Lew wasn't holding out. He had a phone in his van. "Dyer? No sign of any surplus falcons. Burabi the Magnifico came home duded up like Zorro. He had the one, his pet. Hour goes by, he leaves in street clothes, without the bird. To his racquet club, a full-service joint where all the gents go. He's still holed up in there, heavy-lifting daiquiris in the bar. They got a band, cuties, the works. Probably put honey in the daiquiris, or fructose. You know."

I said I did, and got Burabi's address, and the racquet club in case I was in a fructose mood.

"You want I should persevere?" Lew asked.

"Yeah."

"I got my bird book right here," Lew said. "And my binocs. I watch the skies." He hung up. I looked at my blood on the receiver, and then at what Allison had dropped on the counter: the little pickled frog. One more call I had to make.

I tried the Tucson headquarters of Game and Fish, and asked for Tom Franklin, who knew about frogs, and I went oh-for-three. The receptionist said Franklin was out in the field, would be in tomorrow, and hung up.

I thought about calling somebody who wouldn't hang up on me. I couldn't think of anyone. I put the frog in the fridge and that joke didn't last long at all. My hands were two sizes too large and felt like all the needles were still in there stinging. Reed Two must be worse off. He had taken a lot more of the needles in worse places. I had never seen anyone stuck by so many. He'd been coated with them. With my luck, he'd crawl off and die before answering any questions.

Or even worse, he'd survive and want revenge. He'd come chewing after me.

Outside something rustled, tapped, rustled. Then again, up against the house. I was standing there like a dope. I got myself moving for the shotgun, another anachronism, single barrel, single shot. Got one into the chamber. He was out there, he'd followed me somehow to finish it. I went quickly into the bedroom and climbed out the window and tightened up going along the side of the house. I was going to blow the son of a bitch clear to New Mexico.

The desert was dangerous with its little noises. I had the shotgun on all of them. Time crawled by. I got tired of it and yelled. Nobody was out there; except for species lower down, or higher up, the evolutionary scale, I was alone. Jumpy. Yeah, that was it: the woodpecker flicked over the edge of the roof and went at the trim, already pocked with holes.

Allison drove in and locked her brakes, got out. "What are you trying now?"

"Hunting woodpeckers."

"If you get one I'll have to take you in."

"That's what I like about the department."

She pushed me inside and finished plucking and bandaging my hands to the middle knuckles. The bloody phone rang. Maybe I should get a receptionist. A British one. Edwina Garrett, who had started all this, said, "I've been trying to reach you. I'm holding a kidnap note on the falcons. They want ransom money tonight. Can you come up right away?"

"I can't drive."

"You get a DUI? Hitch a ride then."

"It might have to be with someone official."

"Oh, her? As long as she understands I'm in charge. You are having a rough time, aren't you?"

26

It was the first ransom note on falcons I'd ever been called in on. Edwina Garrett had found it tucked in the mailbox at the end of her driveway just before noon, when she went out for the regular mail. The note didn't carry a stamp and hadn't been mailed. Somebody had made the delivery in person—it was sparsely settled country, where that wasn't a risk.

FIVE THOUSAND OR NO MORE FALCONS. CASH AND MAP TO BRUCE CADY. BY HIS LONESOME TONIGHT AT 8. NO COPS NO DETECTIVES.

The letters, crazy styles and sizes, had been cut out of magazines and glued to a sheet of plain white paper. Glued below them was a fragment of a topo map with a stretch of Forest Service road circled. The envelope was also plain.

"What do you think, there's going to be a return address?" Edwina Garrett asked. "What can you tell me?"

"Whoever it is doesn't like verbs."

She snatched back the note and the envelope. "I've called Bruce, he's on his way. What they charge for a hospital room these days, nobody stays in any longer than they have to."

Allison asked, "Why's he named to make the drop?"

"Because he's a wimp, I imagine. He won't make trouble. That's what I called Dyer for."

She was feeling dramatic and a little desperate. She didn't

cheer up while I explained how I'd almost, but not quite, recovered the falcons a few hours earlier.

"I thought you did this for a living," she said.

"I didn't figure on the two guys dropping in with shotguns."

"What's all this about?"

I started to tell her. She interrupted. "No, no, no. Don't give me cockamamie theories about blackmail and murder. Falcons; that's what I'm paying you for. And don't waste your time investigating Bruce. He isn't capable of serious crime."

"What kind of crime is he capable of?"

"He's what I said, a wimp, and that puts him in the clear. Didn't you say this Lupe Jackson and Reed whatever-number-he-is had the falcons out at this camp? Isn't it plain they sent this note before you rousted them?"

"They could have. Frankly, I doubt it. They seemed busy with other schemes. And they weren't literary types."

"You're impossible."

"I just don't settle for the obvious."

"Well, we might have to, if it's true. I don't know why I listen to you anymore. You've had two good shots at the falcons, and you've come up empty-handed." She looked at my bandaged hands. "You came up with a handful of cactus. This case won't be listed on your résumé, I presume." She shook the ransom note at me. "You should be paying it, not me."

"My advice is that nobody should be paying it."

"Well, here's my advice: keep your advice to yourself and do the job you were hired to do." But the possibility of not paying interested her enough that she said, "It'll either be the Jackson woman or Reed out there expecting the money tonight. One or the other, or both. She had the falcons last, didn't she?"

"We don't even know that the person who sent this actually has the falcons."

"I'm not willing to chance it. Does it seem likely that

someone not involved would think I'd pay five thousand to ransom two falcons?"

"No. It is kind of farfetched."

"And I hope I stay farfetched to the day I die."

I told her I didn't mean anything by it. "This bird-napping isn't a professional job. If we don't pay, whoever it is might come back with a lower offer. By stalling we'll have more opportunity to find out who's behind it."

Edwina Garrett slumped, as if the possibilities exhausted her. "This has gone on too long already." She could have been talking about her life. Suddenly, she looked that old.

"I don't like waiting," she said. "I never have. I want the falcons out of that box. I'm going to pay. I've already been to town to get the money. It'll just about drain me dry, but I might as well spend it on this. All it will mean is living in poverty starting next month instead of next year."

Allison said, "What about your land? You could borrow against it, couldn't you?"

"I won't sell a square foot of it or borrow against it. Once I'm stiff it's all going over to the Nature League and I want no encumbrances on the deal, no bankers horning in. I want it kept in one piece for the plants and the animals. I want it to be a sanctuary." The word had special meaning for her. "A sanctuary," she said again. She retreated into her thoughts.

I roused her with a call for strategy. "You said you wanted me to make trouble. What kind?"

"Follow Bruce out there and make sure he doesn't do anything too stupid," she said. "He's capable of it, despite all his education. Or should I say because of it. Keep your eye on him and the money. Don't involve yourself directly unless you see a chance, a good chance, to get the falcons without paying. If it doesn't look good, just come back. Don't jeopardize the falcons any further."

Allison said, "I'll have to drive him."

"As long as you don't interfere. You can be one of those government observers. You can keep your Brucie-boy safe, and you can back up Dyer if he needs it."

"That makes it all worthwhile," Allison said.

We went inside and looked at the last of Edwina's cash, trying to get comfortable on the furniture that had the look and feel of unimpressive archeological finds. It was styled for a lost civilization and sagged from the weight of bodies that had long since been buried. On the walls were brown-toned photos of miners doing it the hard way. One of them was a close-up of old T.G. himself, with his Zapata mustache and the overbearing brow and eyes he'd passed on to his daughter. The glass was broken and there were bullet holes in the photo. I didn't ask.

"All this talk about money," Edwina Garrett said. "I'll probably end up owing you more than I already paid. Got you wondering how we'll settle up after all this is over?"

"How, or if," I said.

"When you can drive you use that old Scout, don't you? You got a liking for old vehicles?"

"Compared to new ones, yeah."

"Take a look at what I got out back." She lurched to her feet. "If there's anything catches your fancy, you can count on that much anyway."

Back in the high weeds and under a spotting of bird droppings, listing on flat tires, there was a '65 Cadillac, a '49 Ford pickup, and a '57 Chevy. They all looked pretty good. The Chevy still had fins.

27

I spread the ransom money on a beaten coffee table and had Allison copy down the serial numbers. It was fifties and hundreds and twenties.

"We don't tell Cady we have the serial numbers," I said.

"Stop giving me orders. I don't take them any better than you do."

Edwina Garrett had lingered out back with the lame or recovering animals she had in cages. We could hear her muttering to them, slipping them food and drink. An altercation broke out between the three-legged raccoon and the coyote pups, with many screamed accusations.

"It's not jealousy making me suspicious of him," I told Allison. "It's facts, and inferences, and the physics of the case."

"What about the physics of men?"

That was Cady's cue to arrive in something Jeep-like from Japan. She went out to meet him, they embraced. I followed and watched them kiss, listened to them murmur.

"You taking notes?" Cady asked me.

"It's okay, Bruce," she said.

"What are you doing with Dyer?"

"It's okay, Bruce," she said again.

"We're working this case together," I said.

"Is that what you call it? You're failing at it like everything else," Cady said. "She just about got killed last night. She probably would have been, if she hadn't saved herself."

His show of anger seemed rehearsed; otherwise he was calm and directed. He had dressed for a safari in one of those vests with Defense Department pockets and pleated shorts and built-up jogging shoes that are being sold as boots these days. He had a felt hat that was the latest thing in ransom-dropping fashion. There was a professional bandage high on his left arm, over the bullet hole, which seemed equally stylish.

"I've got the money," I said.

"Are you banking for Edwina now? Where is she?"

"With the animals."

"She never takes a break, does she?"

As if she'd been listening, Edwina Garrett marched around the house and joined the insult fest. She said to Cady, "You sure got all duded up."

"I better get going," Cady said. "There isn't a lot of time." Allison had brought out the cash, snapped a rubber band around it, and he put it in a pocket that seemed designed for it. He shrugged at me. "I was as surprised as you are that they picked me as the go-between. Maybe they've heard I do good work. Find them and ask them."

I showed him the note and the bird-nappers' map. The road marked was out by Redington Pass, a saddle between the dominant mountain ranges, the Catalinas and the Rincons.

"They picked a good place," I said. "It's national forest land and a few ranches and old mining claims. Just a handful of people use the road on weekdays. It could come down anywhere in this ten miles they've circled. There'll probably be some sign or indication of where you should stop and what you should do. Maybe another note with more directions."

"I had that much figured out," Cady said. "Where will you be?"

"Allison and I will trail a few miles behind. We won't be able to keep you in sight. If you get instructions to turn off, throw this out on the road so we'll know where." I gave him a nondescript block of two-by-four, about nine inches long, that I'd fished out of the woodbox by the fireplace. "Once you make the drop, just drive back here without giving any indication we're on your tail. We'll stake out the drop."

"I'm a little uneasy about this," Cady said. "If they see you, they might call it off. They might take it out on me."

"We can risk it," Edwina Garrett said. "The other side is, you might need some protection yourself."

"Dyer won't be much help from that far back. And what's with your hands?"

"I'll be there too, Bruce," Allison said.

"Of course, hon," he said. "I guess I'll be covered, then."

I had questions for him, about a lot of things, but just by asking them I'd be revealing what I knew or suspected. The next couple of hours might provide answers. I didn't want him changing or doing it differently because of what I might think.

"Good luck," I said.

He looked at me squarely. "Fuck off," he said.

He hugged Allison again and cranked up his thingama-Jeep and putted away.

"You see what I mean?" Edwina Garrett said. "The only crimes he's committing are against himself."

"Why are you so cruel to him?" Allison said.

"I know his father. Guillermo is different. Shouldn't you get on the road?"

"Yes," I said. "Let's go, hon."

Allison and I drove east and then south, circling the Catalinas, on pavement and then gravel and finally rocky dirt. The sun had been low and got lower, disappearing behind the mountains, which were hulking up, we were so close to them. The road was dip after dip, each crest higher as we climbed to the pass. We hadn't seen Cady in some miles, or the two-by-four block that was our signal to be alert.

Allison didn't bother with me. She just drove. She had a sheen of sweat on her face and defining the line of her jaw and down her throat, and her uniform was wrinkled, dirty, with a torn pocket. She really was well made. She looked at me.

"Should I speed up?" she asked.

"This is fine."

We caught up to the two-by-four, lying half on the shoulder, where a lesser dirt road turned off and wound around a cattle tank. I got out, found the tire tracks, said, "Yup."

Allison took the turnoff and went into four-wheel as the road deteriorated and demanded more of her attention. We bumped around the tank and down a long slope and across a rocky shelf in low-low. The vegetation was mostly juniper, stunted trees that seemed greener than they had any right to be, spaced far apart on sparse grass. The Rincons swept up in front of us, the Catalinas behind. Before the Rincons there was a severe drop into the narrow valley of the Tanque Verde, an intermittent creek that drained both ranges. It was rugged land.

Dusk had sneaked up on us. In a half hour we wouldn't be spying on anyone without a searchlight. At the edge of the rocky shelf we stopped. What was left of the road dived toward the Tanque Verde, which was still a good mile away. If we went down, we'd be exposed to anyone in the valley or overlooking it. We didn't have to weigh the decision. Cady's truck was parked a half mile down. He was hiking off to the west.

"Pull back," I told Allison. "We'll make a lower profile."

"Yup," she said. She did it and shut off the engine, and we walked to the drop-off. Cady was hiking away at an angle, using a flashlight that seemed a little premature. A couple hundred yards from his vehicle he stopped, then went on, changing direction slightly, as if he were checking a map or orienting on landmarks. He stopped again at a leveled clearing that dropped away into mine tailings. In the center of the clearing was the opening to a shaft. Cady squeezed through a fence, shined his light down into the shaft, stalled around, and made a show out of dropping something in.

"Very neat." I said.

"He threw the money into that hole," Allison said.

"That's what it looks like."

"What's so neat about that? It's just an old mine. Anybody who comes for the money, we'll spot them easy."

"We can't see the money, we don't have it covered," I said, watching Cady. "There could already be someone down at the bottom. There could be other exits from the shaft, other routes to the surface or to other shafts. Usually there are. Abandoned mines are all over this country, some of them connecting. We can't cover all of it—there's dirt roads and hiking trails crisscrossing this valley, up into both ranges."

"So whoever it is is going to get away?"

"That's what it looks like," I said again.

She picked up on it. "What are you thinking?"

I didn't answer. Cady hiked back to his little truck, turned it around, and crawled in our direction with the headlights on. Before he passed us it was dark.

28

Cady's headlights careened up the slope and disappeared.

Left with just me and the night, Allison was jumpy. "How about a little recon?"

"It's hard enough to go bushwhacking out here in the daytime. We'd need lights, and anyone around would spot us. Let's give it an hour or so."

We crouched against the front bumper of the pickup, studying the valley below, what we could see of it, the contours.

"Bruce was frightened," she said. "This isn't his line of work."

"What is it with you and him?"

"He's fifteen years younger than you and he has all his hair and he's great in the sack. Just the best. He sends me into ecstasy like no man ever has. Is that what you want to hear?"

"Probably wears colored underwear."

"Everybody does now, Henry."

I got out two foil packages and gave one to her. She ripped it open, saw the shape of the cold bean burrito I'd packed from the stash in my fridge. She started eating without comment. For that alone, I thought I still loved her.

"You wouldn't like him even if I wasn't involved, would you?" she asked. "He's just too proper. That it?"

"He's a white man," I said. "That's how Lupe Jackson would put it."

"She sounds eloquent." Allison made an angry noise with her tongue against her teeth. "In that sense, Bruce has to be white to do his job. That's the world we live in. The Nature League, even you have a hard time quarreling with what they do."

"I don't quarrel with the League. We need more land set aside, more protection of every aspect of the environment, because it's all going. Even the worst ones will admit it: they wake up in the middle of the night sweating. They see the end, they just don't know how soon it'll arrive."

"With a speech like that, you should be parading around in a robe, toting a hand-lettered sign."

"Too public. I thought you liked a serious man."

"Some of them," she said. "Nobody's perfect. If Bruce is bending the rules even a fraction and you bring it out, it'll do damage to the League."

"Bending rules?" I laughed. "What rules might those be?" She said nothing. "The League can survive all of us. If he's dirty, he can't do his job and he's got to be taken out."

"You asked me what I see in him. He never laughed like that, Henry. He doesn't go around in a black cloud and he doesn't see everyone the way you do, as half-empty. He has hope and he inspires it in others. All you have is disbelief, and you inspire no one." She stood up. "Should I explain any more?"

"If you'd like."

"Give me credit for a little passion, you bastard."

The ratchet of the night insects tightened around us, and from down in the valley an owl who-whooed.

"I'm sorry," she said.

"No. You're right."

"I lost my temper. I was convincing myself. I've done a lot of that since I left you. I tell myself I miss your twisted sense of humor. I miss how you let go for any wind blowing clouds. And how you can handle yourself. And when you do act on the few things you try to believe in, you're the freest man I know. But you never let anyone get as close as I have to get. You're a loner and you're invulnerable and goddamn you for it."

She turned away, I caught her gently, held her. She said, each word a nail driven by a hammer. "Tomorrow I am putting on a white dress and I will marry Bruce Cady."

I didn't have it in me to tell her, don't. I let her go. Nothing else happened in the hour we were out there.

Finally I said, "If anybody's going for the money, they're somewhere we can't see them, or they know we're here and they're waiting us out."

We had a jarring ride back. The road seemed rougher and longer now that we were traveling without the ransom money or word on the falcons, or anything left to be said between us.

Back at Edwina Garrett's place we had to meet her eyes. The creases around them had deepened and resembled the land out by the Tanque Verde. "*Nada?*" she asked.

"*Nada,*" I said.

Cady showed us a second ransom note. Plain paper, more of the crazy magazine letters: CADY THE SIDE ROAD ONE AND SEVENTH TENTHS DOWN. PATH EAST TO MINE. MONEY DOWN THE SHAFT. IN TOUCH SOON. Glued below the orders was another cutout of a topo map. Someone had marked the path to the mine in pencil dashes.

"They had it tacked to the fence by the turnoff," he said, "where I couldn't miss it. I couldn't see bottom in the shaft. A bunch of broken-down timbers and rocks and dirt were clogging it at the top, but there was an opening, and below that it looked clear. It slanted a little, toward the creek, I think."

I asked, "Was the money naked?"

"What? Oh. I put it in a pouch. A blue nylon pouch with a zipper."

"Good thing you thought to bring it."

"I carry all sorts of gear in the back of my truck," he said. "Be prepared. It's the old Boy Scout motto."

We ticked away two more hours staring at the cracked plaster walls and the fading photos of miners and the shot-up one of old T.G. Only the four of us, and we couldn't keep out of each other's way. Allison wasn't talking and Cady sensed something had happened between us and that added to the tension.

"They'll call," Edwina said, again.

"They should," Cady said. That was his role.

Edwina had us drinking the bitter Mexican beers. The empty bottles were like accusations. She began to ride Cady.

"Threw my money down a mine shaft," she told him. "Down a damn mine shaft. You really handled it for me. Maybe it's fitting. That's where the money came from in the first place—a mine. Now it's gone home. That what you figure, Bruce?"

"I just did what the note said," he told her.

"Well, hooray for that," she said. She jammed a bottle between her lips and got rid of more of the beer.

I had disbeliefs to act on. I excused myself, said I was going out to get some air. A black sky full of stars glittered down on me. I managed to snap on a flashlight and searched Cady's truck. In the glove compartment he had maps, none of which were topos with incriminating pieces cut out of them. Dirt clods and fuzz under the seats. A rolled sleeping bag and a poncho and other camping gear in back. I fondled the sleeping bag as best I could with my fingertips and felt nothing inside. Nothing in the ashtrays or clipped to the sun visors or wedged up under the dash. I popped the hood and crawled under the truck and found two oil leaks and caked dirt. No rubber-banded bundles of five thousand in cash. I was less than satisfied.

I went back inside and Edwina said, "That's it. I told you I'm not any good at waiting around. Company just makes it into torture. You all clear out now. I won't have you moping around here all night. I'll let you know if I hear anything."

"Either the money's gone by now or it'll be there in the

morning," I told her. "I'll come out and rope down that shaft and take a look."

"You can't do any roping with those hands," Allison said. "I'll do it."

"Right, right, right," Edwina said. She hustled us out the door and closed it without saying another word. A moment later the house went dark.

Cady gathered Allison in his arms. "I was worried about you. I had all kinds of scenes in my head, like another fight, shooting. I was about to come looking."

"Nothing happened," she said flatly.

"Let's go home," he said. "You should take some time off. Tomorrow's our day."

"I'm tired," she said. "I have to give Henry a ride."

"He can drive himself. He can sleep here. Then he'd be handy if there's a break."

"Go ahead," I told her.

"Why, thank you," she said. And then, "No, Bruce. I need sleep. I need this one last night for myself."

I walked off to let them settle it. "I'm just tired," I heard her say again. He got miffed and drove off.

She stood where he'd left her. The night seemed desolate. The animals out back of the house were stirring in their cages, the coyote pups started up. There was no moon, but they didn't need one. They yipped away. Then something else, a larger animal, began to howl back there with them. Mournful howls that even so sounded like a celebration in the face of everything.

"It's Edwina," Allison said.

We were violating the old woman's privacy. She was entitled to howl. We left in the Game and Fish pickup, drove down into greater Tucson, depending on who got asked, and then west toward my place. Outside the city the cool air was flowing down off the mountains, rivers of cool air in the dry washes. They flowed every night. Allison thrust her left hand out in the breeze, cupping it, fighting its force. She had started to cry silently, with just her eyes. She said, "I never

132

get over how cold it can be after it's so hot in the afternoon."

She found my driveway and bounced us to the end of it. The engine idled. We had a moment on the balance.

"Allison." I reached for her and she jammed on the horn, held it like a long scream. She let up and in the sudden silence said, "It's too late for that."

"Sure." I got out, closed the door, walked. She turned the pickup and started out the driveway. I was back where I'd started, alone with the night.

Her headlights did a one-eighty and she drove back in my direction and parked and got out wiping her cheeks.

"One last fire, Henry," she said.

We carried mesquite logs from the woodpile to the fireplace inside the courtyard. She crumpled newspaper and arranged the twigs and then the logs. The wood was dry, a benefit of the desert, and the flames took hold. We had the bottle of bourbon. We sat on a pew and watched the flames and their reflection in the old TV screen, passing the bottle, leaning against each other inside an old Hudson's Bay blanket as we had so often before. The local contingent of coyotes started howling and inventing their own noises in their mountains behind the house; it was a night for that, and maybe we answered them.

29

The phone woke us. We untwined on the pew and I felt my way into the dark house to the kitchen, where the ringing was loudest. I lifted the receiver and heard Lew Santiago say, "Four A.M. He's on the move." Lew hung up.

I switched on the bug light for the courtyard and in its yellow glow Allison sat up, bare-chested above the blanket, squinting, raking fingers through her hair.

"Blast," she said.

I began to dress, awkwardly with my bandaged hands.

"Was that Edwina? Has she heard anything?"

"It was Lew Santiago. He's watching a guy for me. A guy who buys peregrines."

"Is there an angle you aren't working?"

"None I can think of. I can't fasten my pants."

"You didn't have any trouble getting them off," she said. "Here." She beckoned me over, did the pants for me and then my belt. "Just like when you were two years old."

"Not quite."

"No," she said. She coughed. "I'm being punished already. You know I'm not a morning person. Tell me it's still night."

"It's night."

She got up modest, wrapping the blanket around her middle, looked at the rind of her uniform, her underclothes on the clay-tile floor. "I can't get back into those. They need a good burning. I'll have to borrow." She felt her way into the house, grousing unintelligibly. I wrestled my socks. She came out more or less dressed, in an old pair of my jeans and my best and oldest gray sweatshirt, one hand securing the pants, the other untangling her hair with my brush.

"I need a belt to keep these things up," she said.

"Only got one." I stood up and she tugged the belt from around my middle. Then she tugged up my socks, put my shoes on for me and tied them. "There," she said. "Don't go crossing the street and don't talk to any strangers."

"Hardy har."

The phone rang again. I listened to Lew saying, "He's gone to ground. The Shangri-La, that motel under the hula girl on Miracle Mile."

"I know it," I said.

"So do I," Lew said. "But you, I'm surprised. He knocked on a room, woman let him in. She didn't look like a hooker. Wouldn't be set up that way anyway. You coming?"

"Sure."

Lew hung up. I told Allison. She asked, "You think they're dealing peregrines out of the Shangri-La?"

I told her what year it was. "Anything is possible."

She wouldn't let me out of there until she'd done a quick change on my bandages. "I was taken by the mummy," she said. "Made me itch all over." I reached for her again, she came into me, nuzzled me somewhat brusquely, said, "An itch, a nice scratch, but that's all. It doesn't change anything."

She ground the gears going down the driveway. She had said she wasn't a morning person.

We hit the outskirts and then the freeway and took it north to Miracle Mile, once the grand entrance to the city. Now there were hundreds of ways in and none of them grand. Some of the old palms still stood tall among the motels that had gone to seed and propagated a neon strip. Women who went with the neon were on patrol in their tight costumes and spike heels. They must have had quotas to fill, to be out that late. They looked at us hopefully, or as close as they could come to it.

The Shangri-La was a low barracks under a pink and green neon hula girl. Oh well. A block-lettered sign on the office advertised rooms by the hour and adult movies. A pair of the adults were checking out at the iron-barred window. She was about sixteen, dressing to hide nothing else; he was a generation removed, with a beery face and attitude. He slapped the pickup as we pulled in, yelled, "Get her."

Allison gripped the wheel. "A little late," she said. Then, "This guy we're after is probably just trying to get laid."

"Al Burabi. He's a Saudi and he drives a black Corvette."

"So maybe he just prefers it by the hour."

The Corvette wasn't in sight. Down at the end of the building we pulled in beside Lew's van, a modified Dodge with vanity handicap plates that said BAD LEGS. The plates let Lew park anywhere, which made him a good stakeout man.

Lew was plunked in his wheelchair on the sidewalk that fronted the rooms. He was dickering with a woman who was simultaneously a blonde and a brunette and a redhead, built like a ferret, with a sharp nose and twenty-pound earrings. Lew rubbed his thumb on her palm. "Come on, sweetheart."

She was playing hard to get, which qualified her for an Oscar nomination. "You're freaky," she told Lew.

That much she had right. Lew was pieced together out of parts of other men. He had the full-size chest of a heavyweight wrestler, arms done in two-thirds scale, midget legs that stuck straight out on the seat of his wheelchair, and a huge head with tiny ears. His head was further enlarged by a wiry turbulence of black hair streaked with dirty gray. There was more of that in his beard, shaved back some to reveal a set of lips that belonged on a concert pianist, the nose of a second-rank boxer, and the eyes of a car bomber. He had put on a tank top with horizontal black and white strips, kid's jeans with the cuffs rolled way back, and little black work shoes, polished so they shined. On every finger he wore a ring laden with some color of stone. In the glow of the neon he didn't look healthy.

"I am freaky," Lew told the ferret woman. "Who isn't?"

"I never fooled with a guy in a chair before," she said. "What can you do? You don't look too good down here." She motioned at his legs and his fly.

"What do you care what I can do?" Lew asked.

"It would be double, at least double," she said.

Lew released her. "I'll have my agent draw up a contract."

She didn't get it. She looked at Allison and me and told Lew, "I'll be around." She walked off sinuously.

"I should've told her I got these legs in Nam," Lew said. "They all go for that, Nam legs."

"Lew," I said.

"Just passing time," he said, "Hiya, Allison. Wearing his clothes again? I thought you gave that up." He worked his eyebrows up and down. "You passing a little time too? Only joshing. Dyer never ventures out on the Mile unless he's on a job. He's a country boy."

Allison said, "These places exist for country boys."

"Country boys, city boys, and in-between boys," Lew said. "Why do they call it the Shangri-La? A victory of the imagination. I can't recommend it. The rooms are cramped and they're done in a sickening green."

"Where's Burabi?" I asked.

"Number seven. He parked around back. They got another lot for the customer overflow." Lew could make a parking lot sound pornographic.

"He met a woman?"

"Not like the others. Heavy-duty Mexicana, face off one of those stone carvings, overdose of black hair, thicker and longer than the lady's here and more like what you'd have on an animal."

"You saw her, what, a few seconds when she had the door cracked?"

Lew shrugged various parts of himself. "Burabi went in, came out after five minutes, dug around in the truck of his car, and dug, and dug. He took a long time packing a little gym

137

bag. Maybe you got an idea what's in it. Just before you got here he took it back to the room."

"She still in there with him?"

"Most likely. She could've slipped out while I was watching him get the bag. But why would she? They had a meet set up."

"She sounds like somebody I want," I said. "Lupe Jackson." I looked around for the Ford pickup she'd been driving, with the load of peregrines, walked around to the back lot and in the mix of sedans and trucks and the black Corvette there it was. The windows had been starred by shotgun pellets, a side one was blown out, and the body had been pocked by more pellets—damage from the blasts the previous afternoon. There were no falcons.

I circled the motel again. Burabi sidled out of number seven. He was still on the leather kick, slick leather pants and leather bracelets reinforcing his wrists. Concealing his pudgy gut was a loose linen shirt that draped outside the pants. His black hair and beard glistened, as if they were oiled leather. More than ever he looked like a creature of the night.

Burabi had the gym bag in one hand. He walked rapidly right at me. His eyes were all over the place. When he spotted me, he thought of running. I braced him before he could. He spit out some Arabic words and saliva. "Mister Coyote Enterprises Unlimited."

I shoved him against the car, did it again. Even though he was soft, I was hurting my hands.

"You were supposed to call me when you got a line on any falcons," I said.

He couldn't stop himself from glancing at number seven. Lew had wheeled up to us. "Hold him," I told Lew.

Lew grabbed him by the wrist and Burabi tried to yank away, then cried out. Without his hunting falcon, he seemed defenseless.

"Don't damage him yet," I told Lew.

I went along to number seven. The air-conditioning unit stuffed in the window squealed for lubrication. I used my shoulder on the door. The jamb splintered and the door burst inward. A ceiling fixture showed up the tropical green walls. There was a swaybacked bed covered by a spread that had started out as yellow, and on the floor, a rug that had started out as orange. Sprawled in the middle of the rug was something that had started out as Lupe Jackson.

30

Bodies talk. But mostly about failure. She had been dead only a little while, her blood thickening in the stab wounds in her chest and belly. A knife with some heft had been used. No wounds on her arms or hands. She'd been taken by surprise, from the front, by someone she knew or considered harmless. It had been painful. She had curled herself around the wounds, clutching them, clenching her teeth inside the red lipstick with her eyes wide open at the end.

The room where she lay smelled of bird residue and there were some downy underfeathers clinging to the rug, but that was it. Still no falcons.

"You want cops?" Lew asked. He had wheeled to the doorway.

"Yeah. But no rush."

"And him?" He jerked Burabi around by the wrist.

"In here." Lew shoved him into the room and left. I couldn't keep Allison out. I wedged the broken door shut. It was crowded in there. Allison eyed the body, then Burabi.

"You stabbed her," she said.

"No," Burabi said. "I did not." Sweat popped out of him.

Bright spots of blood dappled the hem of his shirt. I yanked them up. "She bled all over you."

He stared at the blood. "She had two peregines. She was

asking twenty thousand. I'd had discussions with her husband. An hour ago she called me, said she was ready to do business. I came here to her room and she showed me the peregrines. I left her to get the money from the trunk of my car. When I came back and opened the door I saw her. She was lying right there."

"What about this?" I rubbed the bloody cloth on his face. He screamed, cut it off, backed against the wall.

"Blood," he said. "What we're all made of."

I wrested the gym bag from him. He watched me take out four inches of cash wrapped in foil. Enough to meet Lupe Jackson's price. I spun him and patted him down. In his pants pocket he had more cash, two thousand or so in crisp but slightly gritty hundreds. Oodles of cash had been running through my fingers, not much of it sticking. This batch of hundreds looked like the remainder of the payoff Lupe Jackson had received from Sax Leonard, what she'd snatched out of the sand and the wind after the fight in the desert.

Burabi faced me. He had regained his composure. I slapped him with the hundreds. "You rubbed into her blood taking these off her."

"I can get by without them," he said. "But if God wishes me to have them . . ."

Other than that, what he said hung together. With the twenty large, it looked like he had come prepared to buy falcons.

"She was keeping the peregrines in a wooden box. Over there," he said, pointing to a corner. "She wasn't taking good care of them. I was eager to buy them from her. But they were gone when I brought back my money. If you want my thoughts, the person who cut her up took the peregrines."

"And if I want your thoughts on who that might be?"

"I was buying peregrines. That's completely what I know about."

Lew rapped on the door and wheeled in. "It's done."

In the copless time that was left I threw a search on the room and Burabi's car and the pickup most recently driven by

Lupe Jackson. In the bathroom I found her purse, which held some crumpled twenties that might have come from the jars she'd had buried in her yard. But none of Edwina Garrett's ransom money and no easy-flick knife that Lupe had been so attached to. It had likely wound up stuck in her chest and then had left with the murderer. Next to the purse was a plastic water glass holding a few inches of water and a rangy stem of delicate blue flowers. Nothing else jumped out at me.

Sirens announced the end of my freelance opportunities. City patrol cars pulled in, their flashing lights a logical extension of the gaudy neon. Uniforms took over, and before long I was dealing with a Detective Connors, a walking ball bearing out of Tucson homicide. I greased him enough to get him to call in Sixto DeGuerra from the sheriff's department. DeGuerra had no jurisdiction inside the city, but he had the background on the case. And he could vouch that I wasn't worth hassling without somewhat better cause.

"Falcons?" Connors said. "What happened to the good old days when people were killed in dumps like this because they were fucking around?"

"This is the kind of intrigue Dyer looks for," DeGuerra said. "Falcon intrigue." He patted his aluminum hair.

"Al Burabi," Connors said. He repeated the name, emphasizing each syllable. "You from back east or something?"

They had Burabi and me in another room at the Shangri-La, one where no murders had been committed, that night at least.

"I'm a citizen of Saudi Arabia," Burabi told them.

"I thought it was something like that," Connors said. "You want to blend in over here, you could go with something sounds more American."

"Like Lee Harvey Oswald," I said.

Burabi smiled. "I already shortened it from Abdul, a name used by too many people in my country for its religious meaning: slave of God. Would you choose to go around calling yourself that?"

"Detective Slave of God Connors," DeGuerra said. "I like it."

"Yeah," Connors said. "My mom would like it too."

Cops.

"You got a reason to be over here, Al?" Connors asked. "A reason to be in Tucson? I mean, other than touring the local attractions like the Shangri-La?"

"The university."

"You a student? What're you majoring in? Western women?"

Burabi widened his smile. "Soil sciences."

"Farmer Al. I thought all you Arabs were into oil?"

"My family is into agriculture. It's far more valuable than oil back home."

"That how you can afford to cruise the Mile in a cherry Corvette with twenty thousand cash in the trunk?"

"It isn't a lot of money."

"I'm awful glad to hear that. How can a guy entertain himself anymore on a lousy twenty grand a night? Then what do you do for real thrills, Al? Cut up Lupe Jackson?"

"I go out to the airport and take off in my Lear jet."

Connors looked at DeGuerra.

"If you want names I can give them to you," Burabi said. "People in Washington. Friends of my family."

"You want to please," DeGuerra said.

"I'm cooperating. I'm in an embarrassing position. But I am not the murderer."

"We'll see," Connors said. He had Burabi taken away for, as they like to say, further questioning.

"The face you put on," DeGuerra said to me. "You don't think he did it?"

"No. You find the knife yet? He didn't have it on him, and he had no chance to ditch it. Mainly, he doesn't have the falcons, and that's what he wanted out of her. Until he had them, he wouldn't have killed her, even for entertainment."

"You got falcons on the brain, Dyer."

"From the smell and the feathers, they were here. The murderer took them, along with the knife."

"So somebody sneaked in here and stabbed her while Burabi was unloading the cash out of his car, and this somebody got away lugging the birds in some box, all in, what, five or ten minutes?"

"The falcons don't weigh anything. They wouldn't have slowed anyone down."

"All this while your pal Lew was rolling himself around out back. Awful good timing, or amazing luck."

"Isn't that how these things come down?"

"It is," DeGuerra said. "Now and then."

"So if we aren't pinning it on Al the Arabian jet-set sand farmer," Connors said, "who are we pinning it on?"

DeGuerra asked me, "Should I tell him?"

"Your theory," I said.

"Not just mine," DeGuerra said. "A guy named Reed Two."

"Reed Two? What the hell nationality is he?"

"Country Western," I said.

One of the uniforms interrupted us with a report on the desk clerk. "She didn't see anything, didn't hear anything out of the ordinary—she claims a stabbing is out of the ordinary at the Shangri-La. She's been busy every single minute all night. Doing what, she's less definite on. She wouldn't have noticed if the department helicopter had crashed into the back units."

"You checking the units?" Connors asked.

"Wouldn't miss it. Going to be a lot of female suspects." The cop shook a loose wrist.

Connors looked at the cop. The cop nodded. Connors said, "I'll join you." They went out.

"Every year attention spans grow shorter," I said.

"That's what you get with this affirmative action," DeGuerra said. "You hire Anglos just because you have to. A hundred and fifty years ago this was Mexico and all the detectives were Mexican. It's been downhill from there." He shook his head. "You still got that face. You don't like my theory either?"

"I call it a theory. I ran into Reed Two out in the desert yesterday. He claimed he didn't do Artie Jackson."

"You expected him to confess?"

I ran it down for DeGuerra. He said, "You just slapped Reed Two with a cholla?"

"Yeah."

DeGuerra huffed, shook his head again. "You finish him? No, I guess not. Not him. Buddy, you better be looking over your shoulder. So he's stuck with cactus and really pissed, he comes over here, takes it out on Lupe Jackson, snatches the falcons. What's wrong with that? Got the falcons in and everything."

"Lupe Jackson was a tough, smart woman. She had scams going with him, but they were falling apart. She was afraid of him; she wouldn't have let him get anywhere near her knife. She would have fought him and there'd be wounds on her arms and hands. It has to be somebody she considered no threat who got in the room, found the knife, and waited for the right moment."

"Don't underestimate Reed's bad-ass potential."

"What about all her cash? He knew she had some, he wouldn't have left it behind for Burabi."

"If he was on a rampage, stuck with all that cactus, he might. I've got a bad-ass and a body and as far as I'm concerned they go together. All you've got is smoke so far. And pardon me for mentioning it, but Allison is out there in your jeans, and so I'd say you're a little distracted."

It was the wrong time of day and he'd been rousted out of bed to look at a dead woman on an orange rug and he didn't want to hear about intangibles. So I stopped trying to tell him.

The law was sick of me and me of it. I went outside and saw the patrons of the Shangri-La being interrogated on the sidewalk. Odd couples, mostly men and women who didn't go together at all. They had only one thing in common, and it would have to be done late at night and forgotten by noon.

145

Allison and Lew had been processed. Allison had gone silent and tense. Lew seemed to be enjoying it.

"I should get out more," he said. "It's a wonderful world."

I told him he might have to be getting out at someone else's expense. "My client is tapped. All I can expect out of her from here on in is a fifty-seven Chevy that needs work."

Lew did his piecemeal shrug. "She got any more like it?" I told him about the other two old classics Edwina Garrett had stashed in her weeds. "A Caddy," Lew said. "Full size, how they used to make them. I could slide in on that big front seat, no trouble. Electric everything. Rig up some hand controls, be riding in style. You see me in that?" He poked Allison.

"I see you," she said.

"That would keep me playing," Lew said. "See if she'll part with it."

"Then stick on Burabi once the cops spit him out. We're still looking for two peregrines."

"Hope nobody finds out." Lew wheeled off to his van.

Allison hugged herself inside the sweatshirt. "What does he do in one of these rooms with a girl?"

"Ask him," I said.

"Sometime I will. How can you count on him to track Burabi twenty-four hours a day?"

"It's his specialty. He's got the van set up for it; he's got food in there, a converter, a potty, even a VCR. His record on a stakeout is seventeen days."

"Seventeen days? Without a break?"

"Lew tailed a guy home, he never did come out, so Lew finally called the cops, turned out the guy died in his sleep the first night. Lew thought he was just being cagey."

"I don't know what I'm doing here, Henry. It's all wrong since what we did last night." She wouldn't let me hold her. "This is my wedding day and I'm out with you before dawn inspecting a body in this horrible place. Lupe Jackson didn't look like a person anymore. Somebody turned her into a carcass."

"Let's get out of here."

Allison drove us away from the Shangri-La. "That flower," she said. "The one she arranged in the water glass. She tried to make her room pretty. It's so sad."

"It gets sadder. I think I know where she got it. Guillermo Cady brought a fistful of blue flowers to the hospital after Bruce got shot. He said they were a sure cure."

"They didn't work for her, did they?" She shot me a hard look. "You won't let it go, will you? Now you want to get to Bruce through his father?"

To the east of the strip the night was lifting. This case was putting me through one dawn after another. Soon the sun would be in charge, and what the darkness and the neon had been hiding would be revealed.

31

We stopped at a convenience store for two coffees to go. While Allison was inside the pole lamps over the lot blinked off in deference to the gray sky. Other customers were rolling in, construction workers two and three to a pickup with their radios blaring identical tunes and disk jockey wisecracks. Stunned and bleary-eyed, they loaded up on buckets of coffee and packages of doughnutlike things. Whistling off to work, it wasn't. They rolled out in a grim continuous caravan, off to build the new Tucson.

One of the two pay phones in the modernistic minibooths outside the store worked, and I got Allison to feed it coins and punch the numbers for Edwina Garrett. Edwina answered on the second ring sounding fully awake and said she'd had no word from the bird-nappers. "Any progress on your end?" she asked.

"Sort of. I'll let you know." I told her about putting Lew Santiago on Burabi's tail and my intention to keep him there.

"I didn't okay that," she said. "How am I supposed to pay for another man?"

"If you're willing, he'll take the old Caddy."

"Take my money, take my cars, bag up the silverware if you want. Just get me results. And speaking of money, if I have to I'm going to check out that mine shaft myself, to see if the ransom is still there."

"Sit tight. We'll be out. We've got one stop to make first."

Allison fired up the pickup and drove us north and east, down along the Rillito River, which had gone dry over the years as the underlying groundwater was pumped up into the surrounding neighborhoods for, among other pleasures, landscaping. Big trees had grown up, treasures worth almost any cost in the desert.

Poplars and cottonwoods, sixty feet and taller with interlaced canopies, protected the aging trailer court where Guillermo Cady had settled. The trailers themselves weren't much, single-wides manufactured back when nobody pretended that style of living wasn't a disappointment. They were angled like rib bones one after the other on tiny lots, but they were well kept, with rippled fiberglass skirts and add-on porches and waist-high fences that were being painted every few years. Guillermo Cady had number 24, row C. The yard was a concert of bushes and ivy and flowers.

"You push too hard, I'll stop you," Allison told me.

The old man was already up and working. He crouched over a flower bed, shirtless, a trowel in one bony hand. The flowers burst out in all styles and colors, pure white to valentine red to velvety purple. Some were the blue pale trumpets that had brought me there.

He straightened up, joints creaking, to greet us. "Allison," he said in his deathly whisper. "What's the matter?"

"Just a bad morning," she said.

He looked at me. "You were at the hospital. When Bruce was shot." He appeared even more ghastly in the sunlight than he had indoors. His chest seemed to be caving in, and the skin was mottled. "I forget your name."

I answered the implied question, but it didn't seem important. He stooped in slow motion, snipped off a flower with his fingernails, held it out to Allison. His nails were long and rimmed with dirt. More of the dirt was packed into the creases of his knuckles.

"For the lady," he said. "It's just a petunia. Aren't you jogging about now? I guess you can take your wedding day off."

"We're working, Guillermo."

"You're out of uniform," he said.

I gestured at the blue trumpets. "You give any of these out lately?"

"You some species of cop, aren't you?" he said. "It's in your voice, the way you stand here in my yard."

"I'm a private detective."

"That's not so bad." He creaked over to the cement porch, where he had a plaid short-sleeved shirt draped on the railing. Birds winged by overhead, a formation of sparrows, a swooping thrush. Gangs of them chattered and whistled up in the trees. He got the shirt on, struggled to do the snaps up the front. It had been washed so many times the collar had frayed. He tucked it into his green work pants.

He said to me, "You here to learn about flowers? I don't think so."

"Flowers, and other things."

"Last time I saw you, you were rushing off to rescue some falcons on a cliff. You're a strange detective."

"A woman was stabbed to death a few hours ago. She had one of these blue trumpets in her motel room. Lupe Jackson."

"Did you stab her?"

"No."

"It was justice," he said. "She's the one who shot Bruce. Got him right in the arm. I'da taken care of her good if she'd tried anything like that on me. I'da put a pair of pruning shears right through her."

Coughs traveled up from the soles of his boots and shook him. He covered his mouth with a fist and turned away. A woman emerged from the trailer, as if she'd been watching us or was attuned to the sound of the old man breaking down. I searched for her name: Maria. I'd seen her in the hospital hallway, a ripe teenager with a seamless face and clipped black hair and a baby on her hip. She put the baby down to attend the old man. The baby began to cry. The old man fought his cough. It was a real opera.

"You better lie down," she told Guillermo.

He waved her off and lowered himself to the porch step and coughed between his legs until the spell subsided. "I'm okay," he told her.

"You have to be outside working, you're going to die outside," she said.

"That wouldn't be so bad."

She did what he had done to her, waved him off, and took the baby inside. The little trailer barely muffled its cries.

"Me and her go at it sometimes," Guillermo Cady said. "We got too much in common to hold grudges. My wife ran off right after my boy was born; same thing with Maria, only it was her husband leaving her with the baby. Just like a bunch of damn Mexicans." He started to laugh, slid into the cough and out again. "So now I got cancer eating me up and Maria takes care of me, and the baby, too, but not for much longer, thank God. Not the way I feel. She yells, but I don't mind. A woman likes to have a man to take care of and most of the time a man don't mind."

He stopped to breathe. His lungs wheezed like a stiff leaky bellows. When he could manage it, he said, "Lupe Jackson came by yesterday afternoon, four-thirty, five, in there. She didn't have her little pistol and she didn't stay very long. I gave her a little dab of color from my garden to cool her out. I do that for everyone. She didn't get stabbed here."

"What did she want?"

"She was trying to wheedle money out of us. It didn't make sense. We got nothing to be scared of."

"I think she tried it once already, in Bruce's office, before she shot him. What does she have on him?"

"What any woman does." He smirked. "She didn't come right out with it."

Allison asked, "Was she seeing Bruce?"

The old man's smirk deepened. "He's got a knack with

women, doesn't he? Like somebody else I know." Meaning himself.

"Answer me," Allison said.

"Whose clothes are you wearing?" Guillermo Cady chuckled. It was a compact version of his cough and went on longer than he intended. When he controlled it, he said, "You won't get me to say anything bad about Bruce. Me being sick like this has been hard on him. It's hard to watch your old man die. I only got a couple months left. I'll see it out right here." He looked around at the yard, perfect as a cemetery. "This chemotherapy bullshit. When it's time to go, it's time to go. Who can pay for it, the machines, the foul shit they want you to drink? Bruce's done a lot. He's sunk every spare dollar he's had into me, into this chest. That's where I got it. The lungs. Sometimes I see him, he looks sicker than me. Then he takes a bullet. I told him yesterday, no more for me. No more. He's starting a marriage, save his money for that."

"Maybe he should be saving for Lupe Jackson," I said.

"He wouldn't pay her a cent. Ask him, he'll tell you."

"I plan to."

My plan aroused the cough and it seized him again. Maria reappeared, slinging the baby, who had temporarily gone quiet. She raised Guillermo Cady by the arm and guided him inside the trailer and closed the door with her knee. Since we'd arrived she'd avoided looking at us.

32

Allison noticed the petunia in her hand. "He sounds terrible," she said.

"He wasn't done talking."

"Or you aren't done asking."

"Are you?" I said.

"I don't believe Bruce was having any affair with Lupe Jackson."

"Neither do I. She wouldn't have gone for him. He was a white man, remember?"

"And so what if he was? He's seen a few other women since I took up with him. We're both adults, and I don't hold him to any standards I don't apply to myself. It'll stop once we're married. We've agreed."

"A blood oath, I hope."

I rapped on the trailer's tinny door. The window was louvered and I couldn't see in. I opened the door to what Guillermo and Maria had for a living room, went in. Noises flitted from the bathroom at the end of the hall: running water, coughing, spitting, their two voices going back and forth. The bathroom door was closed. The furnishings around me, rug, and paneling had faded to a shade of brown, the color of earth three feet down, where people are buried.

Propped on a budget end table was a framed poster of the

Virgen de Guadalupe, Mexico's maternal saint. Pressed under glass on the wall behind it was a family photo spread, color shots of Guillermo and Bruce Cady in the yard and in the mountains and one at the beach. And older black-and-whites, of Bruce as a kid with a healthy father. Guillermo had been a strapping rawboned man, before the bite of cancer. The old photos showed him planting a wispy tree, raising an irrigation gate, trimming a row of bushes. In one he was paired with a woman who had a determined look. She stared at me through the decades. Edwina Garrett. She had mentioned knowing Guillermo Cady. She had cried. They were standing in a sunlit field in the faded photo, her in riding clothes, him dressed for digging. They weren't touching, but they seemed aware of each other. I found another photo of the two of them, posing in front of a building I recognized—the old Corner Café in Silver City, a town just over the New Mexico line I'd often visited for its high-elevation relief from summer heat. The New Mexico photo was blurry, and I couldn't make out much except that they'd been there together.

Maria interposed herself between me and the snapshot history. She had quick moves, an exhausted expression. "You leave him alone," she said. "He's suffocating."

"I need a few more minutes with him. He'd want it."

"You need. He wants." She smelled of sweat and baby excretions and other aspirations. She had put on makeup and then it had washed almost entirely away during her chores. Her clothes were for nightclubbing: border-town designer jeans, a black imitation silk top, wrinkled and damp, suspended by straps and showing some skin. She was already rounded out and slipping past pretty at eighteen or nineteen. Barrio eyes, black and strong. "You're in my house," she said.

She stared at me the way women who've been left stare at men. I went around her and down the hall.

Guillermo was propped in bed on top of the covers in his soiled pants and clean shirt. His boots had been removed to reveal his socks, and it hadn't been such a good idea. He was playing with the baby, a bulgy-eyed boy born with more hair than I ever had. Guillermo said his name, Tomás.

"This kid cries all the time. He goes around with a bellyache. Colic; you know what that is. But at six months old he knows a hell of a lot more than most people ever do. He knows to yell when he's hungry or wants to be held or when he's deep in his own shit. A lot of us older folks aren't that smart."

I jumped him. "How did Bruce take it when you told him Lupe Jackson had been by?"

"Like a man. He was angry." Guillermo paused, eked out a smile. "I never said I told Bruce anything. You want me to say he went out and stabbed her? People I know have sons who would have. I almost wish Bruce had it in him."

"Why?"

"Because then he'd have to call off this wedding." He broadened his smile. "Oops, I shouldn't be saying that either, should I?"

"You said it before, a little more subtly."

"He's old enough to decide that for himself. He's picked out a beautiful Anglo gal. Maybe I wouldn't have picked her out, but I won't be around long enough for my opinion to be worth much of anything." He coughed; intentionally, it seemed. "You're beginning to sound more like a regular detective. I liked you better before."

"Have you had much contact with regular detectives?"

"No," he said. "Never."

I shifted tracks. "We seem to have a mutual friend. There's a couple of photographs out in your living room of you and Edwina Garrett. She's my client on this job. It's her falcons I'm trying to find."

"I thought you rescued the falcons."

"Those were the babies. I'm still looking for the parents."

"You might look for a long time. Lots of babies around without parents."

"Did you used to work out at her place?"

"More than thirty years ago." He didn't want to remember, and then he couldn't stop himself. "I was the gardener for her family. The Garrett ranch. They never ran a lot of cattle. Old T.G. wasn't a cowman; he didn't allow cows on his land. That's why it's still in such good shape today. He went around like a king and he got his way with the cows and with Edwina and everyone else."

"What do you mean?"

"Once he made his mind up, that was it."

"And he made it up about you?"

"He fired everyone who ever worked for him; one day he got around to me. I'd been working his land for five or six years and he told me to be off it in one hour or he'd send the sheriff after me. He had the power to say that. So I went. I never been back either. I hear she's still living up there. It's all overgrown now. The plants I put in, the work I did, wasted."

"The cottonwoods are doing fine."

"In back of the house?"

"They've taken over."

"They don't need tending once they get to be a certain size. Up there against the mountains they get a little more rain. That's the only reason they could look good now. She's let everything go."

"In the photo you seem to be getting along."

He thought it over. "We got along," he said. The simple statement was too potent. He watered it down. "She wanted to learn things about my work, and she'd get right down and do it with me. Some of those trees, she planted herself. Once in a while we'd go riding. T.G. stopped that. He didn't want her to go around with a Mexican gardener. So I left. It wasn't so bad."

"Were you dating her?"

Guillermo laughed the laugh of a young man. The coughs overtook him. When he could talk again he said, "What do you think? You've seen her. How does she look now?"

"Pretty good," I lied, "for someone in the desert."

"She's a few years older than me." He shook his head slowly. "She's giving all that land away. She tell you that? She doesn't take care of it, except to keep people off, and now she wants to give it to strangers. There's people she knows who could do a lot with that land. It's good for growing."

The baby had become jealous of all the attention I was getting. He began to squall. Guillermo patted him and the squalls only got louder. They drew Maria. She snapped up the baby and hugged him to her chest. "Tomasito, Tomasito."

"I told you before to go," she said to me. "You don't let Guillermo rest, now you're making the baby cry. If you don't get out I'll make you." She was on the verge of hysterics, the result, I thought, of being trapped in that trailer with the other two as much as with me. The baby cried.

"He's hungry, I bet that's it," Guillermo said. "You better take off and let her feed him. He's still on the tit."

"Good-bye." Maria made it a command.

"Don't get on her bad side," Guillermo said. "That one yesterday did, and hooh-boy, she barely got out of here in one piece."

Maria and the baby backed me into the dirt-colored living room, where Allison was waiting impatiently.

"Don't come around here again," Maria said.

"It's his job to be like this," Allison told her.

"He should get another job."

I said, "Lupe Jackson was pushier, wasn't she?"

"It's up to me to fight the battles for this house," Maria said. "She comes in here making threats, trying to get her hooks into Guillermo and into Bruce and upsetting the baby. Like you, only worse. A woman off the streets. I threw a jar of orange juice at her. I was all night cleaning it up. I think it's good she's dead. You won't hear me regretting it."

We had been raising our voices until we were shouting over the baby. The thin-skinned trailer resonated with the cries. Maria got spooked. She stared at the baby. At that moment, she looked no older than her age.

She said, "I can't stop him from crying."

33

After nearly twenty-four hours with Allison, I had to get free. Maybe she was right—that was about my limit, even with her. But I was groping toward some answers she wasn't going to like, and there was still the little matter I hadn't pursued, of how she'd been mixed up somehow with the punk rednecks, Reed One and Two, slipping them leg bands for their illegal birds. I still didn't accept her explanation entirely—no explanations are that good.

"Well, did you get anything out of that?" she asked once we were back in her pickup.

"A few things. They need solidifying."

"That Maria, she's got guts, doesn't she? Trying to take care of the old man and the kid, and for what, room and board and a few bucks a week?"

When I didn't respond, she let it drop. It turned out she was ready to be free of me. "I've just about had it," she said. "I'll help search for the ransom and then you're on your own. Nobody's ever had a wedding day like this."

"When's it official?"

"Sundown," she said.

"Ah yes."

She didn't like that either and drove the rest of the way to Edwina's place without speaking to me. I was used to it. We didn't waste any time with Edwina, who had nothing new, or getting out to the mine. Allison roped up while I tried to peer into the shaft with a flashlight. She took the light and clambered down onto the timbers and dirt clogging the opening.

"That stuff could come loose," I said.

She ignored me and picked her way through the jumble and dropped into the darkness. Her light played on the walls and got smaller and then I could see only the black hole. She was down too long. Then she was climbing out, standing beside me, dust on her knees and hands, holding a dusty blue nylon pouch.

"I found this at the bottom," she said. "Unzipped, no money. There was another way out. A tunnel took off south. I crawled to the end, it comes out a couple hundred yards down the slope, I couldn't see you because of the tailings. I crawled back through and looked around some more."

"It was that dusty, you see any tracks?"

She didn't want to answer, or to admit to implications. "I'm not too good at reading signs."

"What would you guess?"

"Whoever was down there didn't leave any sign I could find. And that's all you'll get out of me, Henry. You think Bruce kept the money, don't you? That he set it all up and just threw down an empty pouch?"

"It's possible, isn't it?"

"No. Not Bruce."

We stopped again at the ranch to tell Edwina, who made a noise like she'd been jabbed in the gut. "Five thousand bucks," Edwina said. "I'm an easy mark."

"Maybe not so easy," I told her.

"Retrieve that money, Dyer, you'll go straight to heaven."

"I hope not quite that fast."

Allison hadn't gotten out of the pickup. She started driving before I was all the way back in. I got the door shut and she took us across more desert that looked anything but heavenly, out north and west of the Tortolitas to the end of the dirt track where I'd left the Scout.

"I'm not too good at this, either," she said. "Now I have to face Bruce and not think about last night."

"Think how simple it would be to call the whole thing off."

"I told you, it's too late for that. You and I just said thanks and good-bye—what we never got around to before. You have to understand that. All your detecting won't affect my love for Bruce."

She said it like love was a possession she wouldn't give up, short of being robbed at gunpoint. Any arguments I had would have to wait until I had something to back them up.

"This isn't just personal," I said. "If it ever was. It's bigger than that."

"Don't fool yourself," she said.

I got out and she said, "Are you sure you can drive?"

"Sure."

She waited to see if I could get the keys into the Scout's ignition and get it started and turned around. Then she stayed in front of me, speeding up, leaving me behind.

I drove with my forearms on the wheel, but I had to use my hands on the sharper turns and for shifting. It hurt, but that just made me in touch with things.

Like what I had heard and seen in the old photos at Guillermo Cady's place, and earlier, dealing with Edwina Garrett.

I hurt all the way into the city, and into downtown, and parked as best I could, which was lousily, with a lot of steel hanging out into the street. My feet were okay, and they took me to the county recorder's office, where I persuaded a clerk I'd persuaded other times and who knew I was somewhat well intentioned to look up a voter registration. All they require in Arizona is the state of birth. Bruce Cady had listed his: New Mexico.

A pay phone in the shade of one of the high-rises put me in touch with the recorder's office in Silver City, two hundred miles east. The woman there had a file-drawer voice and said it was policy not to answer any requests by phone. I worked on her and discovered the dimensions of the policy were wall-to-wall and floor-to-ceiling. So I tried Silver City's weekly newspaper and got an editor with an understanding of snooping and the value of twenty bucks wired by Western Union. The cost of living and snooping isn't high in Silver City. My feet took me four blocks to the wire office and I sent off the cash. When I called him a half hour later, as arranged, he had the dope: Bruce Ignacio Cady, born such and so in the Grant County Hospital, father Guillermo López Cady, mother Edwina Cady.

Edwina Cady, Edwina Garrett. So she'd taken up with the gardener and mothered a son. And then blown them off.

I had that one hard fact which fit in somewhere and I had outlines where other facts would fit. All I needed was the somewhere and the others. There was a bank clock in view that hadn't stopped three years ago and wasn't telling the time in Hong Kong: I had less than five hours to the wedding. As is too often true, the quickest strategy was confrontation.

I hurt my hands some more getting unparked and over to the Nature League office and parked again. The glass that Lupe Jackson had shot out of the door had been replaced by plywood. Inside the office there was a young woman with a college look: comfortably idealistic. "I'm a volunteer," she said, making it a paragraph.

She told me Bruce Cady had gone off to a luncheon at the Desierto Lindo resort. "It's a banquet for the developer up there," she said. "Sax Leonard. He's getting an award for environmental awareness."

She became aware of me and my bandaged hands. I didn't look too idealistic. "Can I take a message?" she asked.

"Not this one."

It was an opportunity. I tried to look even less idealistic and told her I was an inspector for the city, sent out to check a report that Cady was living in the building, in violation of the business zoning, section three point two subparagraph D.

She trailed me into the back rooms, but when I held up a pair of Cady's underpants as if it were damning evidence, she retreated to the office. There weren't many places that would hide the evidence I was really searching for. One variety I found: taped inside the base of a bust of John Muir was a Ziploc bag of some unnatural greenery, twenties, fifties, and hundreds, a couple thousand worth. Part of the ransom on the peregrines.

34

North of the housing battlefield at Desierto Lindo was what they call the destination resort. It had been rushed into existence the previous winter, in time to be the destination of southerly migrating snowbirds and their dollars. The main building owned a hill by itself, behind a false front of concrete pillars and a massive drive-through porch. They had fountains and fine-tuned plantings, and rippling high overhead in the hot wind, more of the Desierto Lindo flags. Elaborate wings of the building, two and three stories of rooms with balconies and wide-angle views, folded down the hillside. Between the wings, a lagoonlike swimming pool glimmered around a rock island, shored by mature palm trees and a master-concept jungle, criminally green grass, umbrella tables, spas masquerading as hot springs, cabanas, and an outdoor bar—the deluxe Sun Belt package, ordered to go and ready for installation anywhere from San Diego to Miami. Tennis courts had been dropped in down on the flats where the golf course took off. On the fringe were the stables and courts for shuffleboard and bocci ball and the other games. They had allowed for everything except the reality of summer in the desert. In the oppressive heat, the place looked abandoned.

Upscale sedans were cooking in the parking lot. I found a space and started hiking. The cement was an extension of the surface of the sun. I reached the shade of the porch and the two Buster Browns making a living as auto valets. They had a golf cart for hauling around very special guests. They gave me the very unspecial treatment. I went past them through the automatic glass doors, barn-size and more polite, and into the lobby, plush southwestern nouveau, carpeting and wall-paper of tamed Indian designs, glass cases displaying models of pueblos and old pots and arrowheads and worn milling stones. Rooms' worth of room. A ceiling that went where no ceiling had gone before. Mostly windows on the far wall, looking out on the swimming lagoon and the city in the distance, where all cities belonged.

I got directions and nary a twitch at the desk, pushed deeper into the place, down a hallway wide enough for a horse race, into a banquet room filled with admirers. Not of me. Of each other, of Desierto Lindo, and of Sax Leonard.

They receded into the distance, table after table of them, arranged around white linen tablecloths set to the max with folded linen napkins and water goblets and double forks all around. Petite arrangements of dried desert plants in the center of each table. All Anglos, very clean, dressing down in cottons and casual shoes. The waiters were Anglos too, especially them. A wink of gold here and there, turquoise, silver, nothing overdone. Murmured conversations, subdued laughter, studied looks. Plates of designer food. A destination brunch.

I went among them. They wore stick-on name tags bordered in green with a mountain skyline. They had lettered in their names and, in many cases, what they represented: groups to save the environment and wildlife and neighbor-hoods, companies that threw up houses and dealt in real estate, business associations, law firms and, inescapably, government at all levels. It was an odd mix, which would have broken into warring camps most days of the week. But this was a day of truce, and forgetfulness, in honor of the man at the head of the room.

Sax Leonard was ensconced on a low stage, sitting in a row

with some others who were in charge of one thing or another. One of them held forth at a podium, going on about Desierto Lindo and what a triumph it was, as the ceiling lights dimmed and a projector began to flash slides of how the desert had been transformed for the better. Gigantic landscapes and shots of the construction and the care that had been taken were cast on the wall, the images lapping onto the ceiling, distorting. They had shots of the wildlife, long-eared bunnies and the like, and of how the trees and high-end cactus had been uprooted and mothered and replanted, and the spring-fed pool preserved for the picnicking of generations to come.

About then I came across a white-haired rustic of the generation that was just hanging on: Edwina Garrett, I knew her as, hunched over her plate, shoving shreds of boned chicken onto her fork with a crust of French bread. She was a splinter in that crowd, aggravated by another of her scrupulously plain dresses. It was a surprise and an inconvenience to see her again so soon, and before I was ready. She shared the sentiment.

"You plant a radio transmitter on me or what?" she asked. "How'd you track me down?"

"I didn't."

"You couldn't have come for the chow. Even with my taster, I can tell it isn't much." She mashed her bread onto the chicken, shoved the plate away, stood up. "Let's hear it." She marched me to the rear of the room, away from eavesdroppers. "Normally you wouldn't catch me at one of these environmentalist teas," she said.

"I'm not looking for you. I'm looking for your son."

She collapsed. I kept her from falling. "Let go of me," she groaned. She made a fist and slammed it into the wall. "That little shit. Did he come whining to you?"

"About what?"

A man stood up at the nearest table and said, "Could you keep it down, please?" He didn't mean the last part. The Desierto Lindo slide show was still going. Applause broke out. Stepping to the podium was Sax Leonard. He launched into an oration about little beginnings.

"I ordered you to keep away from Bruce," Edwina said. "I didn't hire you to investigate my family."

"It often comes to that."

"The only reason it could is if he stole the falcons."

"He might have."

"He hasn't got the guts. Look at him."

Bruce Cady and Allison Crews were winding among the tables and toward us. They both had on shorts and knit shirts that coordinated nicely. Maybe it was just my mood. Allison, in the lead, asked me not at all nicely, "What're you trying to pull?"

"Keep it down," said the man, who'd lost his *please.*

Edwina gave him the finger. "I'm not getting into this," she said. "Dyer, you're close to being canned. You can salvage it by for once doing what I ask." She waved that imperious stare over me and marched back to her seat and locked her attention onto the show at the podium, where somebody was handing Sax Leonard a plaque.

Cady forced a smile of amusement. "I think your client just gave you the finger."

"She's giving the world the finger. Starting with you, right?"

His smile faltered. "Whatever's bothering you, we better talk outside." He led us out a side door to a patio that somebody had thought needed a goldfish pool and no shade trees. Allison stood beside him.

"I have a motive for him now," I told her. "He's Edwina's son. It hasn't been a model relationship."

"So I'm guilty?" Cady cried. "Of what?" He was trembling.

Allison blazed. "I know all about Edwina," she told me. "Is that all you can come up with?" She reached for Cady, but he grabbed her wrists, turned them up to fend her off.

We stood there under an unsympathetic sun. Words crawled out of Cady like ants in search of better shelter. "I came out of her womb. That's where it ended. She didn't want me—she would have aborted me if Guillermo hadn't argued her out of it. Even then she only went ahead because she could throw me in T.G.'s face. He couldn't stomach a lower-class Mexican putting it to his only child. He tried to have my father killed. He sent men with guns out looking.

"They ran off to New Mexico," he said. "She did it just to be wild and then hightailed it back to T.G. and the ranch a few weeks after I was born. My father brought me up without so much as a postcard from her. Now he's dying poor and she sits up there on a couple thousand prime acres that she's going to leave to posterity. She had the gall to call me up one day after all this time and ask me to set up the transfer to the League. What was I supposed to say? No? I demand a few acres for myself, for my father, to make up for your thirty years of negligence? They never married—they just put on an act in New Mexico—but we make a real family, her and us, we all have this love for the land and if I hear it put that way one more time I'll puke. She can capitalize on that and barge back into my life. She's T.G.'s daughter and she doesn't bend. And I am her son. So you found that out, Dyer, what the hell does it mean?"

"Bruce, stop it," Allison said. "You don't have to tell him anything."

I took out the Ziploc of ransom money, tried it out on him. "It means you held up Edwina for the five thousand ransom. And you did other things."

"What things?" he hissed. He looked cornered, ready to break, and he might have, except Allison was a witness.

She twisted her wrists free. "You didn't do it," she said.

He stared blindly at her. "I held up my dear old mother. It runs in the blood."

"You tricked her out of her last savings and you tricked me."

I shouldered past Allison, asked him harshly, "What else runs in the blood?"

"She's getting off lightly. T.G. set her up for life. I have people who need it a lot more than she does."

"Who was in on it?"

"Nobody. My father has this Old World sense of morality."

"Is he the one who needs the money?"

Cady smiled bitterly. "You want a reason for everything."

Allison pulled him around. "What else?"

"That's all. I faked the ransom note and pocketed the money. She owed it to me, and more."

"You should've told me all of it," Allison said.

"You wear a uniform."

"So that made it easy to lie to me?"

"No," he said. "It wasn't easy."

"Let's hear about the other uneasy lies."

He was good. He got her hands back in his and looked in her eyes and said, "There haven't been any. Not to you. I love you."

I felt like clapping, bad hands and all, but I thought the cheap shot would arouse her anger at me instead. Even so, I had to regain the attack, and when I did, ultimately it had the same effect. "I found the leg bands she got for you, Cady, they were out at Reed Two's camp. They prove you're tied in with stealing the falcons—and with the killings."

He kept his eyes on hers. "I understand why you think the worst of me. I've made some mistakes. But only because of who I am, who I started out to be. You've helped me grow so much already. Don't pull out now."

"I can't think with you touching me," she said. She got her hands back and turned slowly on me. "If you want to bust anyone for those bands, bust me."

"I gave them to the Reeds," Cady said. "It's not her fault. I was trying to trade for the falcons."

I said, "That's pretty weak."

"Sometimes the truth is," he said.

Didn't I know it.

"You've done some real work on this case," Allison said.

"Don't spoil it by making accusations that go farther than the facts."

I looked at her. "You've done the same on other cases. It's one method. Remember?"

"I can't say whether I'm going to go ahead and marry him," she said carefully. "But the harder you push me one direction, the harder I'll go the other way."

She didn't have to say the rest: Cady needed her; in the present context, at any rate, I didn't.

A man was watching us from the doorway to the banquet room, not one of the Buster Browns, not the one who wanted quiet. Somebody who was too interested.

"Let Edwina press charges," Cady said. "It'll only expose who she is."

"I have to work this out," Allison said. "But you need to do some more thinking too. Bruce had a secret and you sensed it and came after him, and you won't open your eyes to any other possibilities. You're still screwed up on me."

"You're making this another test for yourself," I told her. "Don't go ahead with it just to prove something."

"You're a good one to judge."

"She told me about last night," Cady said. "I was wondering when you'd try this."

That was all I could take. I went inside with them riding drag behind me. The man watching us had faded away. We surrounded Edwina Garrett, history coming due, and I dropped the Ziploc of cash on the table in front of her. "There's a couple thousand there. Your son had it. He says he just scammed you for the cash. You can ask him for the rest of it."

"I guess he'd have the guts to do that much. Let him keep what isn't here. It's worth it to be rid of him." She stared straight ahead. "Now go get my falcons."

Cady started to laugh.

The program with Leonard had gone along. From the podium he spotted Cady and called to him over the loud-speaker, "There's the man who put it all together for us,

Bruce Cady. The famous biologist. He kept the ecology in one piece out here. In a few hours he's getting married out at our Panorama of Rocks."

Leonard ordered Cady up to the front to take some of the credit. They stood together, Leonard with his professional smile, Cady blinking and looking a little stunned. Leonard and Cady.

I was making fists out of my bad hands and it hurt.

35

I left the fiesta at Desierto Lindo. The man who'd been watching me all along came out on the porch to finish the job. One of Leonard's, I thought. Like the duo with shotguns that had helped put the cactus holes in my hands. Now that I knew all about who begot whom, I was down to solving Leonard. He was probably the reason for a lot of unpleasantries.

I sweated over that and the steering wheel, driving faster than I wanted to back downtown. I'd identified one motive in the case: Cady evening the score with his mother. There was at least one more motive, having to do with Cady and Leonard and Desierto Lindo.

I had to start with what was on paper. I parked in the concrete burrow under the county complex and rode the elevator ten floors up to the planning offices where the real money got decided, where every new pack of houses and apartments and shops or even something grand like a Desierto Lindo got the thumbs-up or thumbs-down. The staffer who handled my request had an average thumb, which probably meant he was down in the middle ranks. He had a name like Putnam. Floppy perm that was too young for his face, open-necked white shirt, jeans, chronic love handles. Anyway, he was trying. Like many bureaucrats, he seemed oblivious to my appearance—I was just an outsider—and complimented that anyone would show interest in his work.

"Standard procedure on Desierto Lindo," Putnam said. "Bruce Cady did the EA—the environmental assessment—for us. We get more work than we can handle in here, so we farm some of it out. Fast as this town is growing, we could double our staff and we'd be just as far behind next year. Cady's one of the reliable freelancers. He knows his stuff, and he's got credentials, his background with the Nature League. Nobody doubts it when he gives a development the okay. Saves us hassles down the line, when opposition mounts, because it always does. Neighborhood activists, no-growthers, eco-nuts, they come out of the bushes beating the tom-toms. Can't even put in a Seven-Eleven anymore without justifying and mitigating it like it was a nuclear dump. If Cady's done the EA, they back off. They respect him."

"How detailed was the EA on Desierto Lindo?"

Putnam liked my speaking his lingo. "I'm using the federal term: it's descriptive for our purposes. You have to do an EA on any development that affects federal land: national forests, parks, BLM—that's Bureau of Land Management. Have to determine the impact. State land is under similar but looser protection. Government owns a checkerboard all around Tuscon. Gets complicated when a developer wants to put together a big parcel like what Sax Leonard did up at Desierto Lindo. He had a core of private land, a dude ranch, scattered holdings. Then he started trading other land he had, or leasing, or outright buying, for the federal and state land that filled in the gaps. Now he's got control of it all. We take a look at every project in the county, and with a conglomeration like Desierto Lindo, the regs require a full examination. The other agencies let us coordinate it out of this office; they just signed off on the report once Cady was through."

"What did Cady make on the job?"

"It's public record. Not a whole lot. He subbed out some stuff to a geologist, other specialists, did the plants and animals himself, maybe wound up with a few thousand out of it. All the agencies chipped in, I'd have to dig for the exact figure. We don't have to bid it up. Buyer's market these days, as far as biologists go. Lot more of them than there are jobs. Schools are turning out more every year. People have romantic notions about the field, until they have to go out and actually try it. We paid Cady the going rate and got a bargain. If Desierto Lindo isn't the biggest project this county's ever seen, it's up there."

"Big for Leonard too."

"Imagine so. He's got a lot riding on it." Putnam got up abruptly and tugged on a cardigan sweater vest that was so bright green it seemed like an escape from something, or everything. It hid his love handles. "All summer they keep it freezing in here," he said. "Got one thermostat for the whole building, they keep the air-conditioning cranked, and there's no windows that open. Hundred and five outside, and I come to work in a long-sleeved shirt."

"Why doesn't somebody do an EA on that?" I said.

Putnam didn't laugh. Maybe he thought I meant the sweater. That's probably why he charged me ten cents a page for a slab of public records: a photocopy of Cady's report on Desierto Lindo.

As I paid him, he asked, "What's wrong with your hands?"

"Paper cuts," I said.

I rode the elevator down and warmed myself on a concrete bench in a little concrete plaza between the high-rises. It took about thirty seconds. Then I was hot again.

I skimmed the report. It was, as Putnam had indicated, fairly standard. There was a description of the land parcels that had made up Desierto Lindo. Maps depicted elevation and drainages and vegetation types, and there were listings of the animals and plants, where they were found and in what populations. Burrowing owls got a mention. Cady had predicted that the graders would scrape them off the land, and that the owls would resettle in reduced numbers. He had noted impact on other wildlife, but none of the species were protected or even rare. For some of the native plants, the quality cactus, he noted requirements or recommedations for special treatment—tagging and boxing for replanting. There was no indication of anything that would cause blackmail and murder. Drops of sweat off my forehead stained the final page.

It was an NSI, no significant impact, the standard finding. Officially, Cady had cleared Desierto Lindo. But somewhere in there was an SL—a significant lie.

Cady had been squeezed over it, by Lupe Jackson and probably Reed Two. They'd also squeezed Leonard, until he sent the shotguns out. She'd given me some vague story about her husband collecting snakes and lizards out there. She'd been saving that little pickled frog.

I had a date with that frog that I'd been putting off too long. It was out at my place. I started driving there, wondering why the hell I had to live so far out—one question I did know the answer to. Then I was bouncing up the driveway and going in and opening the fridge and looking at the frog lying on the top shelf. It was still pickled, and keeping its secrets.

I took the frog out into the courtyard to make a closer inspection under sunlight. It was maybe three inches long, olive green, mottled on its back. The formaldehyde dripping off it got into my bandages and made my hands sting. I dropped the frog and was trying to make my fingers pick it up when a shotgun exploded around front. It sounded like the front door had gone. Somebody kicked open the remains.

"Oh please please save me." The high freaky voice put on by Reed Two. "Oh help. Oh help."

36

I had a second or two, and no guns at all—they were stored elsewhere in the house, or in the Scout. I hadn't been carrying because my hands were so bad. He clomped into the living room, using not much but a little caution, all I rated. I didn't even have another cholla to bat him with. I got my fingers around a screwdriver off the workbench. I wasn't going to do much with it against him, or with anything short of major caliber. He clomped into the kitchen, I folded in behind the angle of the wall, he clomped on back into the bedroom. "Come out come out wherever you are," he said in that freaky voice. The outside walls of the courtyard hemmed me in, rough adobe as tall as the house, and with good hands and a little more time and no need to be quiet I could have climbed them. He'd catch me before I got over or he'd be waiting on the other side. "Ally ally oxen free," he squeaked. "Oh please don't hurt me."

There was maybe one place. I tiptoed to the behemoth old TV and slid it away from the wall, holding my breath, and knelt down inside the cabinet and tried to draw it back around me and back against the wall. There were no innards or picture tube, just the glass screen clouded by dust and scratches and smudges, and through it I could make out the courtyard and the doorway to the house. I had no room to hunch to either side or below the screen and if he looked hard enough at it he'd see me. Or he'd figure it out some other way and just put a few shots into the cabinet or drag it off me and use his hands or his teeth.

He clomped into view and into the courtyard. "Oh please," he squeaked. "Oh please."

From my low and confined angle he looked bigger than ever, his left arm wound with dirty gauze up under the shoulder strap of the bib overalls, half his face taped with pads. He moved stiffly, as if there were more bandages under the overalls. It didn't make him seem any more human. He aimed the shotgun, a pump-action, around the courtyard as if it were a sniffing dog. The TV and I were against the south wall in shadow and maybe he wouldn't see the screen that well. The shotgun and his eyes got to me, lingered, and then roved to the other wall and around. "Oh Henry," he squeaked. "Come on out and play." He made another circuit with the shotgun and clomped back inside the house and fired at something. I took another breath.

He clomped around in there and then outside around the perimeter of the house and the courtyard walls and fired the shotgun a couple more times, "Red rover red rover let Henry come over," and fired again and clomped back inside and right into the courtyard. He sat down heavily on the rear pew with the shotgun on his knees and wound up facing the TV and me. I stared out of my box at him. My idiot box. Maybe he could see me even in the shadow and through the scratches and any reflection off the screen. Maybe his eyes were bad. Maybe he liked my show. Maybe he'd get an urge and try to turn the set on and then what? I could do a fair but dated Walter Cronkite.

He raised the shotgun and aimed at me. My series was being canceled. "Dow dow," he said. Slowly he swung the shotgun away, aiming at other things on the walls. "Dow dow, dow dow."

He rolled to his feet. "Henry come back come back," in his freaky voice again. He clomped into the house, stayed a while longer squeaking to himself, and clomped out where the front door had been. I took another breath.

I stayed hunched inside the TV for some time, twenty minutes, forty minutes, three days. But the sun never did set. Then I took another breath and slid the cabinet out and unknotted myself and stood up. My hands were complaining again; I'd been clenching the screwdriver and trying to support myself in that awkward position. I sneaked into the house and got my ludicrous single-shot shotgun loaded and some shells and looked for him. He'd shot holes in some furniture and windows and the side panels of the Scout and left a note on the hood, finger-painted in blood: CACTUS HENRY YOU SHOULDA STUCK AROUND SEE YOU SOON LOVE REED TWO.

The blood had oozed out of a woodpecker that he'd impaled on the radio antenna. Probably the same woodpecker whose tapping had made me nervous the other day. It had been my joke, but he'd followed through—he'd shotgunned it. I got a knife and cut the little corpse off the antenna and gave it an under-the-nearest-rock burial.

In all his clomping around he hadn't clomped on my pickled frog. I retrieved the frog from the floor of the courtyard and started out in the Scout, staring over the bloody scrawls on the hood, watching for him.

37

The Tucson branch of Arizona Game and Fish had escaped from downtown out into the first rise of the Tucson Mountains. The new building was a pink one-story square, clay-tile roof, square of desert around it, with a laminated wooden sign. The natural look in bureaucracies. Inside was a room where the public was served: low shelves of pamphlets on hunting and fishing, a bulletin board pinned with posters against littering in the woods and drunken boat driving, a counter where licenses were sold, behind it the ubiquitous desks and filing cabinets. What they call trophies on the walls: big-daddy fish stuffed in mid leap, sawed-off heads of deer, antelope, and javelina, and the peeled skin, stretched out head to tail and paw to paw, of a somber-eyed snarling mountain lion.

I hadn't been around much since I'd quit the department. The receptionist had come after my time and was content to leave it at that. She buzzed Tom Franklin and he appeared at the security door, a grainy and totally bald man with a uniform that looked like part of him. He ushered me into his office, walled with photos he'd taken of desert wildlife, photos that had required long stalking and patience, and on his desk, a photo of Louise, his wife, the one that got away.

It was a cramped room and there was only a single chair

behind the desk. Franklin halfway sat on the desktop and I did the same. "Who you been fighting?" he asked.

"Everybody."

"Sounds like you."

I took out the little frog and put it on the desk. He picked it up, sniffed it, said, "It's starting to go bad. Should be in some kind of preservative, there's damn few of these around even in this condition. Where'd you get it?"

"A lady's purse."

Franklin snorted. "She have a thing for frogs?"

"I need a positive ID."

"Hell, it's a T-frog, Henry. Not quite full grown. *Rana tarahumarae*, the Tarahumara frog. mostly found down in Mexico, in the canyons where the Tarahumara Indians live, wiped out in this country eight, ten years ago as far as anybody knows. Still carried on the T and E list, in case any show up. How'd this gal get ahold of one?"

I told him a little bit about Lupe Jackson and her scumbag associates, and Desierto Lindo.

"Desierto Lindo?" He sniggered, shook his head, repeated the name derisively. "You think they found T-frogs out there and then kept it quiet? The Tortolita foothills—elevation runs, what, twenty-seven, twenty-eight hundred? Peaks up to forty-six? It's not impossible. You'd need year-round water; a pretty good stream, or a spring, something that'd create pools that'd last all summer. Anything like that out there?"

"There's a spring-fed pool in a wash. Had water in it a few days ago."

"If it was holding water in June, probably does all year. Odds are against it, but if there were T-frogs in that pool, it'd surprise a lot of people. Well, maybe not a lot, but everyone familiar with the species. And it'd sure hold up the development. They couldn't do anything that'd put a T-frog population in jeopardy."

"They made the pool an ornament. There's hiking paths, the golf course goes right by it."

"Just what we need. Once this desert is all used up, we can

write on the certificate, 'death by golf course.' I guess Arizonans could get into blackmail and murder over promoting another golf course." Franklin lifted the little frog and turned it in the light. "He's a handsome fellow, now, isn't he? Too bad he didn't get a chance to breed. You want my T-frog rap?"

"That's why I came."

"Not something many people have the details on, even in the department. No glamor in studying or saving amphibians. T-frogs weren't even located in this country until the thirties and then only in the mountains south of here: the Pajaritos, the Atascosas, some in a canyon off the Santa Ritas. By the time we noticed them, they were already dying off, and I hear they're even in trouble down in Mexico now. T-frogs are a primitive and delicate species that can't adapt. They're the only silent frog—they don't have a voice worthy of the term—and they spend most of the time hiding. Very specific needs that are hard to meet; mainly a home pool that never dries up, like you get once in a while in a canyon stream or maybe marginally from a spring. They're stuck in the tadpole stage two years, way longer than other frogs, and that's their big weakness. That's how they got wiped out down in Sycamore Canyon. Some fool fisherman introduced sunfish, and the sunfish went after the tadpoles, and that was it. No more T-frogs. They just don't compete well, and people made it harder on them. Like when bullfrogs were brought in. As many bullfrogs as there are now, they aren't native. They were introduced all over this region and down in Mexico years back, as a novelty food and to accommodate the frog hunters. Game and Fish stocked bullfrogs everywhere we could think of. The bullfrogs went after the T-frogs, ate the tadpoles and adults, squeezed them out of the habitat, and before long all we had was bullfrogs in most places, and no T-frogs at all. Eventually we wised up and launched an official bullfrog eradication program—you got dragged into it, didn't you, Henry? Sitting in the bushes with a BB gun and trying to thin out the bullfrogs a little, to right a mistake we'd made and make room for the native species. Only it was too late for the T-frogs. Peña Blanca Canyon used to be thick with them, and then it was dammed to make a lake, bullfrogs and fish were dumped in, and the T-frogs disappeared. Upstream at Peña Blanca Spring there was another pretty good population, but then the spring was walled with concrete and a lid was put on, and a pipe outlet so the campers would be able to get a drink easy, and so much for the T-frogs."

I sat there feeling tired out by everything. Franklin looked at the biggest photo on the opposite wall: a mountain lion carrying off a young deer in its jaws. "I was on a team that studied one of the last colonies, over in the Santa Ritas, but they died off before we got done studying them. We'd hike in and find T-frogs strewn all over the banks, or floating upside down, or sunk down to the bottom of their stream, dead, or paralyzed, their legs straight back like they were ready for little coffins. Their nervous systems had short-circuited. In the final stages they'd get terminally stupid. They'd decide to swim across a pool underwater and just forget what they were doing, try to breathe, and drown. They'd sit on the bank and forget they needed to get wet every so often, and they'd just dry out and stiffen and sit there until they died. It was a mystery as compelling as any you've taken on, Henry. Finally we figured out what was causing it."

"We were," I said.

Franklin nodded. "Circumstantial, but the evidence pointed to air pollution. A combination of copper smelters and car exhausts from Tuscon and Phoenix—hell, Los Angeles and Denver, Mexico City, Tokyo, it's all one sky anymore. Heavy metals in the emissions were collecting in the sediment in the pools: cadmium, arsenic, chromium. Toxics that kill in funny ways. Then the double whammy: acid rain generated by the same sources was eroding more toxic metals out of the canyon rock. Same thing got a bunch of Japanese years ago on the Jintzu River, I think it was. People in convulsions, acting crazy, with like a runaway cancer that made their bones grow right through their skin. They called it the itai-itai disease: the ouch-ouch disease. Cadmium in fish they ate. The T-frogs got hit just as bad, but in their nerves and basic cell functions. They died every way you could think of, all over their range. That was the end of them in Arizona."

Franklin reached deep into a drawer and brought out photos of the little frog corpses in grotesque positions, littering a canyon stream.

"How could any have survived?"

"A remnant population, isolated like what you're imagining at that pool, might be explained a lot of ways," Franklin said. "Something in the soil or the water might be reducing or neutralizing the metals. Could be the drainage or precipitation pattern. Give me fifty thousand in tax money to look into it, and I might be able to give you an answer."

Frogs, I thought. This was supposed to be about falcons.

38

There was legwork to do on the frogs. Franklin left it and the bad jokes to me.

"I can't rush into Desierto Lindo making charges like what you've got in mind, accusing the city's darling developer of collusion with the Nature League rep," he said. "Even if I sneak in, somebody spots me and it'd have the same repercussions. One of the League's directors sits on the game commission. My boss eats dinner at his house. We've always worked closely with the League. You're still just guessing, and even that would upset people and smear the League and maybe cause some of its backers to pull out. A couple deals we've all put a lot of work into, to save some critical habitat, could be scotched. Cady's been the front man for the League down here. He's untouchable until I have more evidence. I should say, some evidence. A shred of evidence. An iota. A flea on an iota."

"Iotas don't have fleas," I said.

"Somebody in the research branch is doing a paper on that." Franklin refiled his frog photos angrily. "All you got right now is a frog in some gal's purse. Even if there was a colony of T-frogs up there, by now they've probably been fucked over by all the construction. They're probably all dead anyway. You get some evidence, give me more to go on, and I'll bust Cady no matter who it pisses off."

"You ever hear of anyone trafficking in T-frogs?"

"Like these trappers you're talking about? No, I haven't, but I'd believe anything when it comes to commerce in wildlife. Collectors would pay for healthy T-frogs. There's guys, rich guys, got their own private zoos, whole rooms and built-in terrariums for stuff like this, and snakes and lizards. They got an affection for creepy-crawlers. And there's others that don't specialize but want at least one of everything that's hard to get. T-frogs would probably fetch a good price. Any market is supply and demand, and when the supply goes down, the price goes up. Some guys would pay a lot more, knowing they were getting the last ones."

"What if I should happen to find myself up at Desierto Lindo, around that pool?"

"Nighttime would be the best, or late afternoon. That's when T-frogs are active, feeding. They won't be sitting around croaking for you; like I said, they don't have a breeding call like other frogs. But you might hear them making what they can manage, kind of a little grunt. The release call. They do it when they get picked up, or crowded, when their home pool shrinks in the hot weather. One time I counted seventy frogs in a pool eight feet across. Go in with a flashlight, shine them. I doubt you'll find any, but if you do, bring me one and I'll take it from there."

I went out the security door, past the skinned mountain lion and the antilitterbug posters, out into the late-afternoon heat. Watching for Reed Two. My hands were throbbing again, I was dry and hot and used up. I started driving, accompanied by images of frogs in little coffins, and my new probabilities:

Cady had discovered the colony of T-frogs and gotten a payoff from Leonard to make no mention in his report. And Cady had brought in Artie and Lupe Jackson to collect T-frogs and sell them on the side. He was cashing in on T-frogs. Then Lupe had tried to blackmail him and Leonard over it. The Reeds were in there too. And Allison. Somehow.

The peregrines were just a tangent. The Reeds, the Jacksons had learned about the falcons from Cady and gone out and trapped them, maybe over his objections. No honor among scumbags.

I lifted the .38 from the glove compartment, tried to hold it. The bandages on my hands got in the way.

I sweated through the city and out toward the Tortolitas, low brown mountains shimmering in the heat. There were no clouds, never going to be any again, no relief from the sun. I drank from the canteen I kept in the Scout. Hot water, tasting of canteen.

Desierto Lindo went for miles. I probed the boundaries, got on a track made by construction equipment through the brush, came to a fence, no-trespassing signs. Strands of wire had been stretched across the track, wound around poles on each side. I got wire cutters out of the toolbox, used them with some difficulty. I drove in, dropped into a wash, and left the track when it climbed the other side. Less likely to be spotted on the low ground. In four-wheel drive I explored the wash, barely wide enough, but sandy and clear of boulders that would have stopped the Scout. It was a meander taking me through hills into the heart of the development. Finally the hills opened up and I couldn't go any farther without being spotted. Ahead was a yawn of ground that had been given the treatment, denuded and leveled and laid out with utilities. I walked out a little ways and got myself located. I turned around, drove the wash into the protection of the hills, then took off cross-country, slipping tires, up a hill to the west, down and around to the bigger wash that led toward the pool. The bottom was studded with boulders that made driving tougher. I got out and started walking. Diesels grumbled, out where the building was going on. I had seen cement mixers, backhoes, and off where houses were being banged out, pickups and carpenters. Down in the wash it was private. Just me and the sun. Gnarly mesquite, suffering from old age, here and there a paloverde. On the banks, greasewood, pitchfork saguaros. Sign of rabbits, quail, javelina. Hard walking in the sandy bottom. I did a lot of breathing. The gun dragged on my belt holster. Around a bend there was the sandy-colored cement path cutting down the east bank, to the ramadas, the pool.

The wash had widened, and I was exposed on the approach to the pool. I got on the cement path, walked faster. There were a few big trees left around the pool, the rest had been cleared. The water was brownish, seven or eight yards across to the overhanging bluff where the manicured golf course wrapped around. The shallows had evaporated, leaving a ring of mud.

I didn't see any frogs. I didn't hear any frogs. I didn't see any frog tracks or frog coffins.

A man in street clothes topped the east bank and strolled down the cement path. He had a walkie-talkie with a little coil antenna. He spoke into it, came closer. It was the one who'd had me under surveillance at the destination brunch.

Another man came over the top and started down. The two of them huddled, halfway down the path.

Time to go. I walked quickly toward them, left the path, and walked by them in the sandy bottom. They were twenty feet above me, the walkie-talkie scratching. They watched until I was around the bend. I started running, not all out, but faster than a walk. It was what I could manage, in the sand, in that heat. I stopped and walked and then ran again, got to the Scout, did nothing else until I had another drink from the canteen.

Maybe I had overreacted. Sure. I heard a truck, it lurched into view, driving the crest of the hills east of the wash. A Blazer. Men inside. The Blazer stopped fifty yards away and a man got out. Chunky Hispanic in shorts and sunglasses; one of the shooters Leonard had sent after Lupe and Reed Two, and inadvertently, me. Happy. With a shotgun. This time it didn't seem inadvertent at all.

I got the Scout going, spinning tires in the sand, banging between and over the boulders. I couldn't turn around, no room and no time. I raced toward the pool and the two with the walkie-talkies. The Blazer, the happy one riding shotgun, stayed above me on my flank. We bounced around the last bend and into the open toward the pool, and the Blazer hurtled down the bank, angling to cut me off. My windshield cracked, cracked again. Somebody kneeling on the path was aiming a pistol with both hands. I wrenched the wheel to the left, missed him, turned inches tighter than the Blazer, almost rolled, smashed into the west bank, bucked up and over and got the Scout roaring up the hill and out of there. Driving over rocks and bushes with the engine raging and the tires clawing dirt and rocks and air. I got to the top of the hill and shifted up and the engine decided not to explode. I was going too fast and the broken windshield made it hard to see and I tromped the gas and got going faster, turning parallel to the wash and almost rolling again on the sidehill and then cutting a line across the hills, flattening anything in my way, holding on to the wheel and pressing the gas and the hell with it. It was a series of crashes, not a drive. The Blazer had come up onto the hills after me, but I was keeping it back there.

"Oh yeah," I yelled. Things like that.

I banged around the cab and my only ideas were about holding on. I flew over a rise, across a dirt road, crashed, wheels down, lurched sideways and yanked the wheel to force the Scout around and up onto the road—potholes and soup-kettle holes and loose rock, bushes growing in the center that I had to run over—ruled by every dip and hump, leading this way and that and west up into the Tortolitas. The Blazer was back there fighting my dust. The mountains came up and surrounded me. The ground dropped away on the passenger side. The road was wide enough for one wheel and maybe the other. I scraped the rock face on my side, the side mirror tore off, the window in the door burst. Way down, below a series of sharp rock ledges, the slope hit bottom in a dry slash of rocks and cactus. The alleged road widened briefly for a little mine dump and some old workings, and narrowed again. It couldn't get worse, and then it did.

I was losing traction. It was all fractured rock, loose and slanting over the drop-off. I gunned it and got across a bad stretch and then it got bad and loose again, I gunned it across that. The road was looping around a mountain of the rock fragments and back to the mine. Dead end.

I thought I might get out and try some shooting, but I kept gunning it to see what happened and skidded around to the end of the loop and suddenly there was the Blazer, crossing broadside, and I rammed it. Everything slammed around and was noise, the Blazer slid sideways, went nose up like a sinking ship, and disappeared. The Scout was going down after it, and I stood on the brake. I had the front wheels over the edge and the rear two on the road and lurched to a stop staring down at the Blazer, its metal complaining as it slowly rolled onto its roof and began to slide on the loose rock. I rammed into reverse and let out the clutch, oh so easy. The tires spun and skidded the wrong way and then grabbed, and I backed up onto the road. The engine muttered and died and I got out. The Blazer was still sliding, wheels up, avalanching the fractured rock, and then it lost momentum and rested that way, on a tilt. The roof was crushed.

39

A man crawled out of the wreckage, pulled another man out. The second one could only sit, head on his knees. The first one started up the slope for me. The happy one with the shotgun, if anything, looking happier than ever. A hundred yards of steep climb separated him from me.

I waved my bandaged hands at him, smiled. I like a man who likes his work. I had a tremor in my legs that I didn't like and then the Scout wouldn't start. They never do in these situations. It's designed into them. The crash had buckled the hood. I pried it up, found where one of the cross braces had bent against the carburetor, caving it in.

I took the little .38 in both hands, aimed clumsily downhill, fired. The shot echoed, raised a puff behind and to the left of the happy one. Not far off. He hugged the rocks.

"Take your time," I yelled.

I got the Scout rolling down the road, pushing it with the door open, and climbed in, not gracefully. The road had enough of a grade. I steered, the Scout picked up speed, I strangled the wheel trying to pick up more. I had to contend with the cracked windshield and the thought that more of them might be coming up from below.

I coasted miles, almost out of the mountains, and then stalled in a low spot, pushed the Scout off the road, down into a crease where it wouldn't be seen by anyone driving by. They wouldn't know where to start looking. I took the canteen and the gun, the Arizona basics, and started jogging parallel to the road, fifty yards to one side. The mountains blocked the late-afternoon sun; I was in their shadow and it was slightly less hot. I had a lead on any pursuit from behind. No sign of anyone ahead. I was coming out into the foothills and could look down on the scrapings and neat layouts of Desierto Lindo.

They had put on a real charge. Leonard couldn't keep everyone away from that pool forever. Maybe there had been evidence out there, some T-frogs or their remains, and he still had to destroy it. Or maybe he just wanted to slow me down, make the intercept, try to determine how much I knew and work out an explanation for it.

Or it could have been totally serious. He could have ordered the murders to hush everything up. I'd seen how he puffed up, getting that plaque for only partially raping the desert. Like an award for date rape.

Or it could have been Cady doing the murders. Or both of them together. Or someone else. Or or or.

That reminded me of the falcons, wherever they were. The thought stuck in me like another cactus spine.

I was losing the advantage of elevation, and the rolling hills hid a lot. Another truck was grumbling up the road. I lay down behind a clump of greasewood. A white pickup idled by on the road, two men inside, Desierto Lindo logo on the door. It grumbled on toward the mountains.

I abandoned the road after that, cutting south toward a destination I had spotted on the maps in Cady's report. I covered a mile or two, came to a rocky drop-off. The sun was going. Below was a peculiar field of eroded boulders, balanced on one another precariously. A group of forty or fifty people had collected down there. Men and women, kids. Their vehicles were parked on the other side, where a dirt road wandered off. Somebody was playing a guitar, flowers were being handed around and sniffed, and there was goodness coming down.

It was what Leonard had called the Panorama of Rocks. The planned site for the marriage of Allison and Cady. They were going through with it.

40

I wasn't that underdressed, it was strictly informal, but I may have been underfreshened. They were more of the spotless cotton crowd I'd seen at the environmentalist tea, well scrubbed, well mannered, well everythinged. All organic ingredients. Some of the kids scampering around actually had flowers in their hair, and nobody was hollering cut it out. I picked my way down and made no stir mixing with them. There was the obligatory flute player. They were sipping clear wine from those disposable plastic glasses that come stacked in a tube, chatting away in little subsets, waiting for the sun to touch the horizon. That was the proper moment. I heard them say it.

They did have a proper site, just enough south of the Tortolitas to have an unobstructed vista to the west. We had a few minutes until the sun got its act together.

Bruce Cady and Allison Crews were west of everyone else, so they would be framed by the sunset when the ceremony began. She had on something simple and white, a dress, with a necklace of coarsely made silver beads, Navajo most likely. Her hair was woven in braids. Her cheeks were glowing. I saw them. He had on something similar. It wasn't white and it wasn't a dress and it wasn't anything Navajo, but that was the idea. His cheeks were not glowing. That's where it all broke down.

I homed in on them but got headed off by someone who wasn't well anythinged: Guillermo Cady.

"You," he whispered hoarsely. His dark subterranean face thrust out of a dress shirt that was sizes too large and had become another symptom: once he'd been big enough to fill it. His string tie was clasped by a curly-tailed silver lizard. "You come here equipped with a pistol?"

"It wasn't thought out. I just stopped in."

"Go ahead, shoot it up. I was thinking of it myself." He clamped my arm with his bony fingers. "But hold on. If it's gotten this far, let it happen. And no more of your questions or dirty business. Not now, not here. To learn about this family, you ask me, and make it tomorrow or the day after. I'll tell you all about Bruce's mother. Don't trouble him with it. I'm the one who took up with her."

"So Edwina wasn't invited?"

"That's not so bad." He coughed, occupied himself with it.

I moved on, but only as far as a fellow dirty businessman.

Sax Leonard was hard to miss in slick black shoes, Mercedes gray slacks, and an ornate light blue guayabera, the Mexican wedding shirt. I got next to him and realized for the first time how small he was under his veneer; I had five or six inches on him. He didn't flinch, it wasn't in his repertoire. He just said, "Don't depress me. I don't allow it at weddings. It's one of my rules."

"I can't help it," I said. He tried to edge away and I stepped on his shoe. "One of your trucks is on its back up in the Tortolitas. I walked out with an emergency message: you've got a frog problem out here. Or you had. People are going to hear about it and see through this Desierto Lindo hype. You'll have to get a new slant on your ads, like, Endangered Species Village, or Thugs' Haven. People are going to wonder just how few rules you have. People like the cops. You can never satisfy a cop."

Leonard sharpened a smile. "Get off my shoe." He tugged

it out from under me. The flute and guitar began a birdsong. "Let's be honest." He draped an arm up over my shoulder and maneuvered me to the fringe, and when I brushed him off he backed against a smooth boulder twice his size, crossed arms over his guayabera, hiding the lacy pleats and embroidery, showing his power jewelry, a heavy gold ring, gold watch. "I thought you were looking for falcons, Dyer."

"I am."

"How much could they be worth? I'd pay to replace them, if that would close out your interest in all this."

"They can't be replaced."

"You speak in absolutes. The world isn't like that."

"It can be."

"You're in charge of the bottom line?"

"When it's thrust on me."

"You got the quote wrong." He snorted. "Shakespeare was talking about greatness. But you know that. It seems like every cut-rate PI is a walking *Bartlett*'s anymore. You could probably give me the act and the scene and the line."

"Sure."

"So okay. Let's say I did have a frog problem. It wasn't much of a problem. But it would have forced me to cut back the acreage up here by twenty percent. That much would have been impossible to develop. It would have been locked up by the feds so these frogs would have room to hop around. And it was prime land, it had water, a spring, you know what that's worth. Let's say I came up with a solution to my problem. Let's say I paid Bruce Cady a little on the side to make my frog problem go away, simply by not reporting it. That's not much of a crime, is it? In the world we live in? You couldn't prove Cady didn't overlook the frogs by mistake, and that's no crime at all. Let's say Lupe Jackson found out about this, and so I paid her too. Paying blackmail, that's no crime. That would make me just another victim in the world of victims. Let's say my security men tried to help out, they rousted Lupe Jackson and her finger-eating partner and got the worst of it. They're just more victims, of some very violent people. Now you tell me there's been a crash up in the mountains, maybe some of my men injured, I guess they were chasing you for trespassing. They're victims again, and so am I. All of this doesn't make me much of a criminal, does it?"

I got in his face, leered. "Let's say you're a murderer. Let's say you had a clear motive to have Lupe Jackson killed. Let's throw her husband on your dead pile too. Now that would be a crime, wouldn't it?"

He recoiled from the charge. "I pay blackmail as a matter of policy. I don't get into murder."

"You make me want to see the staff manual."

"I might draw one up. It would explain that I'm a man with money who has the potential to make money for those around him. That's all. Some people try too hard for a piece of my action. They get a little crazy—on their own. Like Bruce Cady or Lupe Jackson, or those men who've been chasing you. I don't have to try hard. I've already made it."

"A little crazy? There's bullet holes in my windshield."

A beeper sounded. It was hooked to Leonard's belt under the guayabera. He switched it off, said, "I'm not out there patrolling the range. I hire men to do that. They take the initiative, try to do the best job they can. Should I blame them?"

"Oh, heavens no."

"You realize how much these frogs have cost me already? My first thought was like yours: market around them. But they were frogs. If they were deer or wildcats or even rattlesnakes it might have gone over. But frogs just wouldn't sell. Now, as you suggest, I might give it a shot anyway. I can't even say if there are any frogs left out there. Can you?"

"Game and Fish will be checking it out."

"So you've made a report."

"In iambic pentameter."

"No use me making you any offer."

"None. Now where are the falcons?"

"You've got me confused with Noah, the guy with the ark. I don't want you pissing all over me when this things goes public. If I had information to trade, I would. Because I can tell you're a trader."

I looked at him, saw what he was: just a self-contained little man who'd been able to keep himself intact over the years, and who would never be anything more. There were thousands just like him. He wasn't worth a punch.

"Sax Leonard," I said. "Didn't he used to live around here?"

People bolted past us. A woman screamed and went on screaming. I joined the race. It ended on some rocks below an overhang. A woman, not the one screaming, was sprawled on the rocks, face down. Her white dress had split up the side and her angles were wrong. A man I didn't know rolled her over gently, and her necklace separated and scattered the old silver beads onto the rocks.

Allison was unconscious, blood on her face, down the white dress, other places. I shoved the man away from her. "Don't move her." I checked her vitals; she was breathing shallowly and had a fluttering pulse.

Somebody else shoved me aside. A blue-jeaned woman who didn't look old enough knelt, said, "I'm a doctor."

"She fell," someone said. "Up there."

I couldn't see Bruce Cady.

41

The land had treated her harshly. I left her in the care of the doctor and a pair of the off-duty EMTs who seem to be everywhere now and climbed around the overhang and up until I saw how it laid out. The side of the hill was nearly vertical, embedded rock shelves protruding. She had dropped off one shelf, five yards or so, tumbled down the slope, then off the lowest shelf another five yards onto the rocks. I found where she had rolled through the shindaggers and other low spiny plants that wouldn't have held her up. The lower shelf hid most of it from the crowd below, and it wasn't likely anyone down there had seen how it began, who pushed her.

The sun was setting in the west, but that was the only thing that could be counted on.

I climbed down the slope, more careful than I had been on the way up. Feeling my age, and brittle-boned. The field diagnosis on her was a long one: shock and possible concussion and possible broken ribs, and maybe other things wrong inside. She had as good a chance as anyone to last a few more hours.

The sirens were closing in. They were never far away, never really out of earshot, not for anyone who listened. It was the full posse: ambulance, sheriff's car, more coming. I had to escape them, escape anything official, or I might just let loose. The right thing was to ride in the ambulance with her. But I had a case. And it was cracking.

I faded and looked for suspects, and I had broad tastes. None of my possibles were around, not even Reed Two—maybe he was against marriage as an institution. Half the vehicles had pulled out, their occupants avoiding trouble, or going off to cause it somewhere else. Bruce Cady's pseudo-Jeep wasn't in sight, but that may also have meant nothing. He was an enlightened groom; maybe he'd carpooled.

The sun had fled over the horizon. The flicking red lights made the precarious boulders dance.

I turned my back and started to hike again, got on a bridle path, recreation for Desierto Lindo. It went the way I wanted to go: north, into the development, toward the pool I'd started for in the afternoon. I still needed a T-frog, if there were any left, to show Game and Fish.

What had been done to her hadn't been planned—there was no guarantee the fall would kill her. It had been done spontaneously, out of emotion.

At least she hadn't married Cady yet. She could still call it off. Maybe more weddings should include one of the principal parties being pushed off a cliff.

The sky held the glow from the city to the south. I had water from the canteen. One thing about the desert, you get thirsty enough and old canteen water tastes like champagne—old champagne that's been sitting around in a canteen.

I could have gone on for years, but I came to the little pool in the desert that was my destination.

I looked down from the hill. Someone was down there with a flashlight. Shining it around the water, the muddy shore. Only one to manage. I crept down the hill, over the bank and into the wash, the sand, where the cool air was flowing. It was easy to be silent in the sand. If whoever it was shined the light my way I'd be caught, or forced into some other tactic. But the light stayed away from me. I crept closer.

The pool was haunted. It stared back at the light and at me with dozens of pairs of tiny orange eyes. Wherever the light pointed, in the pool, or on the edge in the mud, it shined on the eyes.

A man was wielding the light. He waded into the mud, stomped on a pair of eyes, extinguished them, stomped on another pair, making frantic noises from deep inside himself.

42

He was stomping frogs. I ran and shouldered him down. He slopped around in the muck, got up slowly like something coming unburied. I had the flashlight by then, and the gun out and on him: Bruce Cady.

"Creatures of the night." His voice cracked, hysterical. "Dyer?"

"Me."

"Allison—she's dead?"

"No. They took her in an ambulance."

He made a noise that was beyond laughter. "She loves me. They all do."

The frogs were grunting around us. The release call: Release us from all of this. T-frog soul.

"Come out of there."

"This is where I belong. In the slop. The primeval slop, where life began. One night it crawled up onto land, and it should have turned around and crawled right back into the slop."

"Don't tempt me."

"Shoot," Cady said. He rushed, hugged me and the gun. "Shoot me," he whispered. I dragged him onto dry ground, dropped him. He lay there, making more noises.

I waded into the pool, shining the light, and they were

everywhere: Tarahumara frogs, their eyes reflecting like some deep and secret energy source. They floated, heads out of the water. They crouched in the shallows and the mud. The light blinded and immobilized them. Some of them blinked it off, jumped into the deeper water and swam down to the bottom, thinking that was security. I picked up one that wasn't as shy, a big one, fist-sized, going maybe a quarter pound; slippery, slimy, but no residue, and nowhere near as drab as the pickled version, fertile brown-green with a pale yellow belly and spots on its back like a felt-tipped pen touched on wet paper. With the strange little hands and swollen thumb pads. It grunted and I put it down, and I waded onto land, where Cady was staggering closer with a couple of five-gallon cans.

I pried them out of his hands, tripped him. The cans sloshed. They were unmarked. I unscrewed the lids, smelled the sweet chemical brew. A pesticide, I guessed. He was going to poison them.

"I should dump this on you."

"No one's going to believe any of this," he said. "Sad little frogs. They're doomed anyway—doomed in Arizona; that has a nice sound to it. That covers a lot. If I don't kill them they'll just die off in a few years on their own. I'm putting them out of their misery. They're lucky to go quickly."

"It's convenient to tell yourself that. They made it this long here, they might hang on."

"Don't give me scientific discourse. We're all dying out in a dead and dying world. Why shouldn't I do something for myself for a change? You want excuses? Goddamn you liberals. I get so sick of you."

I grabbed him, stung my hand slapping him. "Don't call me a liberal. How big a payoff did you worm out of Leonard?"

"Ten thousand dollars."

"And you wanted another five from Edwina? How did Artie Jackson get involved?"

"We had an arrangement."

"What?"

"Anything he'd have a buyer for, he'd pay me to locate a

specimen. Gila monsters are up to a couple hundred now. Then I netted him a dozen frogs and he turned them for real money. He wanted more; I told him no. I thought the frogs might survive here if we just left them alone, some of them might live through the construction, and maybe someday someone else would realize what they were and then they could be protected. I thought the colony might make it. Jackson didn't know where I was getting them, not at first. He made threats. That's why he trapped the peregrines—he thought it would force me to cooperate. As if I cared what happened to Edwina and her land." He curled inward. "But I did care. He was voracious."

"And when he got killed, Lupe went after you, thinking you did it."

"He was dead and all she wanted was money."

"Wasn't that what you wanted?"

"To help my father, and . . . I was starting a marriage."

"You'd already soured it, by corrupting Allison. You got her to supply leg bands so Jackson and the Reeds could disguise birds they'd taken illegally."

"Yes." He made noises again.

"And now she's in intensive care. Who put her there?" I shook him.

"I did," he said. "I did it all. I killed all of them."

"You shoved Allison too? I wish you had. You wouldn't do it, not to her. The peregrines. Where are they?"

He told me that much, and we started out, lugging the poison.

43

The streets of the city were lined by oversize garishly lit signs with little or nothing behind them. I'd been gone too long, or maybe my mistake was in coming back at all. We were in Cady's simulated Jeep—he was driving under my gun and swinging from one extreme mood to another. He hit the horn at a Buick that was trespassing in our lane. "What do they say?" he said. "A species a day gets edged off the planet?" He hit the horn again, a tinny sound. "I'd like to edge that one off."

He drove us to the little trailer in the rows of little trailers under the big trees. In the darkness all the careful plantings in the yard seemed ominous. Nobody answered my knock on the door. Locked. No lights showed. "I'll break it down," I said loudly. Guillermo Cady opened up and showed me a rifle, an Enfield from a couple wars back.

"I don't care what you do to me," he said. "I'm dead anyway."

"In a dead and dying world. Your son already tried that line."

I started in, he worked the bolt action. We stood like that for a while. I said, "You don't have enough bullets for everyone who's coming, old man." The baby cried somewhere behind him.

We went in past him. The baby was throwing tears in a basket on the couch. A candle glowed under the poster of the Virgen de Guadalupe. Maria walked slowly out of the bedroom with a knife. She held it in her fist, down at her side, blade straight out. The baby cried harder.

"Don't, Maria," Bruce Cady said.

"You tell me nothing," she said.

"Please," he said.

She shook her head. Her dark eyes were all the way open, her lips pulled away from her teeth. She stabbed air with the knife. "Get away."

"She'll do it," Guillermo Cady said. "She's not bluffing."

She cut off a thatch of her hair, then another one, throwing black handfuls down in front of Bruce Cady. "What do I have to do?" she asked him. "You want a blonde? Does this help? Is this what you want?"

He reached for her, she slashed his hand, drew blood.

"Stop that," I said. I had the .38 out.

"Save myself for what?" she asked. "For him? For a man who makes love and whispers things and makes a baby, and then goes off with someone else? Just because she went to college and won't embarrass him?"

"I love you," Bruce Cady said.

"You love everyone. You love too many people. I killed for you." She stared at the knife. "The first time I don't even remember. I hitchhiked over there. I was going to tell him to lay off you. He showed me your mother's falcons. He started bad-mouthing you. He grabbed me and said he wanted to do it, ever since he used to come over here. He was rough. Then this detective shows up. I had to hide in back and then I was driving away in his truck. I think about it sometimes and I can't remember but it's hard to think at all with the baby around. Then when I'm doing dishes or picking up after the baby or hanging laundry out, I get this flash and I see it like on TV. He had a knife like they cut open boxes with at the grocery store and I used it to cut him open. I opened up Artie Jackson. This isn't the knife. This knife I got later on. From his wife. Her I remember perfectly. She came into this house telling all about her schemes, how she wanted you to meet her with money. I got her to say where she was staying. I went there at night and knocked on her door and started talking and got the knife out of her purse. She acted tough and she didn't make a scream or anything, but she wasn't as tough as the knife. I stuck her and stuck her. Then I took the falcons so you could give them back to your mother or do whatever the hell else you want to do with them. I made it right for you and for us and then you go ahead with this marriage to the other one. Blondie. So I went there today and called her out. She didn't make a scream either. I think my ears are going too."

The baby cried.

"You run out on me and the baby. You know what it's like to have a baby inside you and push it out when there's no man to help you take care of it? You know how it feels to let a baby suck on you all day and keep it with you all the time and when it cries there's no one but you to pick it up? You know what it's like living with the crying and crying and crying?"

She picked up the baby, held us off with the knife. "None of you know anything about it," she said. "*Tomasito. Mi pobre Tomasito.*" The baby quieted in her arms.

Bruce Cady made his laugh noise. "What a picture. The nap-time killer. Slipping out while baby's napping to slit a few throats."

"I'll slit yours now."

"You might as well. You already did, without the knife. While you were doing all this for me I was wrecking myself for you and the baby. What an exchange of gifts we've had." He grabbed the knife blade, cut his hand, drew back and stared at the blood. "You wanted it. You got me between your thighs and had the baby to keep a hold on me. You want to ride me out of the barrio. There's a pattern in this family and you're part of it. My mother slept with the gardener and I slept with the maid. This generation repeats the last. I thought at least I could give you a start with money and that it would make a difference. Of course it doesn't. I am my mother. Thirty years ago I was that baby. I see that now. But you're part of it, and so is he," pointing to his father. "What did he tell you? That I'd suddenly see the light and come home to you?"

"I hoped you would," Guillermo Cady said. "Before the blood started flowing."

"It started a long time ago. It's just breaking to the surface now. My own mother still cares more about her lousy javelinas than she does about me."

Guillermo Cady shoved his son with the rifle. "You blame it all on her. You never even knew her. You see this baby, what this mother feels, think how it was for her. It destroyed her to leave you. She sweated and screamed to bring you into the world. You think it was just the lady in the big white house lying down with the gardener? What do you know about it? I'm a man and she's a woman and we were together. We would ride up into the mountains. We would make our own trail. We would see the sun coming up and there wouldn't be another person for twenty miles around, no one but us. She loved the sun, and she loved anything green. She could read a leaf the way you read your papers; she could tell what any roots needed. And she loved the dirt, and digging out the rocks, she would get down with a pick and a shovel and a pry bar and work all day in the same hole with me. And then together we went on the run. She had courage and great heart and great trouble. What do you know about any of it?"

Maria swung the knife. "The hell with thirty years ago. You whine about all this stuff and then you turn me in."

"Give me the credit," I said.

I had seen a lot of killings. All along I'd been thinking these had the look of women's work, done quickly and quietly from in close. And I was always suspicious of babies.

"I should have turned you in," Cady said. "I should have gone right to the police after the first one."

"Why didn't you?" she screamed. She lunged at Cady with the knife, backed him to the wall. She moved in, I raised the

.38, Guillermo Cady the rifle. We were aimed all over the place, poised.

The baby cried, the same cries that had resonated all through the case.

"The baby," Allison said. She was at the door, in a hospital gown, bandages here and there, an Ace elastic binding her ankle. She limped between us, bare-assed, got in beside the knife, looked into Maria's black eyes. "The baby," she said again. Gently she pried open the fingers around the knife; it dropped on the floor.

Allison glanced at me, then Cady. "I got out," she said. "All the way out."

Maria hugged her Tomasito. I felt like apologizing. All Maria had killed were people. I was busting her for it and I still didn't know her last name.

And I wasn't quite done dancing. A guy with the look of pavement stuck his head in out of the night: Allison's cabbie. "Very exciting," he said. "But the meter's running."

I paid him off and then poked around the place, followed by Guillermo Cady and his rifle. Out back in a screened porch was the plywood and chicken-wire cage the falcons had been in. It held droppings and a few wispy feathers.

"We never wanted to be in the falcon business," Guillermo Cady said. "Had no plan once we got them. God sent somebody to take care of it. Big ugly guy came by this afternoon pumping his muscles, wanting money or anything he could turn into it. Acted surprised to see the falcons. Said they were his and took them. He was strange, wearing more bandages than either one of you. He gave me his number: two."

44

I had my hole card. I used the phone in the trailer to call Lew Santiago. He answered on the first ring. "Dyer. Been trying to get you. The cops let our boy Burabi go. He's been making the rounds, went home, packed a bag and got his bird-in-the-hand, dropped it off at some house. Just got out to the airport, still cruising around, away from the main terminal, looks like he might be making a midnight run in that jet he has."

"He might be meeting a peregrine salesman first. Watch for a monster guy wrapped in gauze with red hair done like Pippi Longstocking."

"What if he shows?"

"Let's hope I'm there by then."

Lew gave me rough directions and we broke off. I dialed 911 and recited my name and location and told them there was a homicide case coming together. "Get Sixto DeGuerra. He'll know what it's about. Send a squad car to nail it down until he gets here." I hung up, faced the others.

"I'm taking the little truck. There's no use in running."

The way they looked, there was no use in anything.

"Too many lies, Bruce," Allison said. She had limped to the door, white-faced. To save argument and avoid leaving her with the three of them, I let her follow me outside. She gave out and I had to pick her up across my arms, and then it was either leave her in the yard or take her in the truck. I laid her on the seat and drove us through the city of broken speed limits and blown yellow lights and failure to yield.

"Why didn't we take the cab?" Allison asked. "That's the usual scene, isn't it? 'Cabbie, there's an extra twenty in it if you haul ass.'"

"Quicker this way," I said. "I'm more motivated."

"Cheaper, too," she said. "You're so damn methodical. It drives me crazy."

"That's how things get fixed."

"This wasn't some broken windmill. It was my romance." She blew out air. "They shaved a spot on my head."

"It'll grow back."

"Not everything does, Henry."

A block from the airport entrance I stopped at a convenience store and called Lew again. He didn't answer. I slammed the phone down and followed what directions and guesses I had.

On the lane to the private hangars an airport cop ventured out of his shack to stop us. I showed him ID, said, "We're seeing off a friend who's flying out tonight. Al Burabi."

He made a note on his pad and waved us in. Lew's van with the BAD LEGS plates was parked on the edge of the tarmac by a hangar. Lew wasn't in his van. Al Burabi's Corvette was parked closer to the hangar, and so was another van, an old VW.

I had a long run across the tarmac to the hangar. Allison was coming slower behind me. Big jets screamed low over us, taking off and landing, their lights strobing, a raw interruption of the night.

Three figures had bunched around a sleek pocket jet outside the open bay door of the hangar. They came into focus. The dark one was Al Burabi, bearded and unkempt in black jeans and a leather vest, taking two packages from the big man, shirtless in the torn bib overalls: Reed Two. Beside the big man, Lew hunkered in his wheelchair. I got up to them, stopped, breathed. Nobody minded.

Burabi was inspecting the packages: the two peregrines, hooded and shoved in nylons, ready for traveling.

I had the .38 on display, but it hadn't done me much good lately and I had no reason to expect improvement.

Reed Two counted money in an envelope with his left hand. He tucked the envelope in his bib pocket. In his right hand he had a .45 automatic that he made look small. With his left hand he grabbed Lew's hair, yanked Lew up in the chair, Lew doing a push-up to go along.

"The cripple your pal?" he growled. He pressed the muzzle of the .45 against Lew's head. "Get rid of the piece or I'll clean out his ears but good.

"Right now," he yelled.

I lowered the .38, held on to it.

Burabi said, "You should have stayed out of this."

Reed Two yanked Lew higher. "I haven't wanted nobody in a long time as bad as I want you. We'll pile in my van and go out in the desert and play around. You, me, the cripple, and her."

Allison had come up off the left and sat down on the tarmac, gasping.

"The piece."

I dropped it. He dropped Lew, swung the .45 to cover Allison and me. "I'm going to turn you inside out. Tack your hides on a board." He stamped his boots, went into his wild man act, panting louder and louder, screwing up his face, thundering, "Pain pain pain."

Lew grabbed, fastened himself to the big man. His wheelchair banged over as he climbed. The two of them strained and the .45 flamed twice, down into the tarmac, as I reclaimed my gun and moved in, looking for a place on the big man to shoot. He began to whirl, cursing, Lew riding his shoulders, shrunken legs flopping. Lew was all tangled up with him. I shot at the big man's boots. The second shot connected and he pitched sideways, grabbed me, and the three of us went down. He had me, snarling and coming with his teeth. I tried to hold him off and shove my gun into him, but he got a hand on it and wrenched it away. He snarled louder. Lew had him in a neck lock from behind and was squeezing. Lew worked on his neck and I worked on staying clear of teeth. The guns were loose somewhere. Lew was choking him good. He let go of me and got up with Lew riding him and began to whirl again. He tried to peel Lew off, beat on him, but couldn't reach. I groped for guns. His bandages unwound in streamers over me. The blood on his boot and on the tarmac was black. Allison had the .38 and was leveling it as I lurched to my feet. The big man's face had turned red. He slowed his whirling, staggered, sank to one knee, got up looking astonished and whirled some more, toppled over on his side. Lew squeezed.

"Amazing," Allison said.

Lew let out a yell. He unlocked himself from the big man, rolled clear, did a handstand and walked on his hands over to his chair, righted the chair, put himself in it. He brushed himself off, straightened his rings. He'd lost one of his little shiny black shoes. He ran his stubby fingers through his tumbleweed of hair and beard. He found the little shoe on the tarmac, wedged it beside him in the chair. I handed him the big man's automatic.

"Not that amazing," he said. "He'll have to get a new number. Reed One Half. Reed None."

The big man cursed, breathing raggedly.

Burabi strolled over to me bearing falcons. "To keep you from shooting holes in my plane, and so your friend doesn't attach himself to the wheel struts, here."

He gave me the falcons. They seemed fragile, weightless.

"They've been abused," Burabi said.

He bent over Reed Two, extracted the envelope of cash. "They're weak and hungry. He said they had liquids forced down them. We treat peregrines better in my country. With respect."

45

We took the falcons to where they had come from. We cut them free of the nylons and the tape on their legs and unlaced the leather hoods and let them go, weak and disoriented. How they would come out of it, if they would, I didn't know. I could have turned them over to Edwina Garrett, to be, ahem, rehabilitated. But they had been in cages too long, and there was something about that word. They would make it on their own or die, and either one was preferable to the cage and the handout and being fooled into trusting humans in any way. We freed them back in under the cliffs where they had nested. The night was dark with a grin of moon and they didn't know what to make of it at first. They stood on the desert floor in our headlights, ruffled and preened and slowly got their bearings. Man, they looked fierce. Then they took off, the female first, lifting herself with some effort and the breeze of her wings, staying low, and then the male, both of them out of the lights and gone. We waited and they didn't come back. There was a dusting of stars high up beyond the cliff, and it was cool and still.

We drove out the old road, paying for every mile, and then up the highway and in the lane to the old ranch house. Edwina Garrett was up, spiting the late hour, looking more imperious than ever. I told her about the falcons and everything else.

"I'm to take your word for it? Why didn't you bring them here to me?"

I just shrugged.

"I've got the fledglings," she said. "Two of them are going to make it. I'll have them flying and back in the wild within weeks. One's too far gone. Wouldn't take to captivity." She brought her full stare down on me. "You figure on your own they'd be rejected by their parents after this long apart? That was up to me. I knew from the beginning you'd be hard to work with. I thought you'd stop short of outright rebellion."

"Guillermo Cady has a saying, 'That's not so bad.'"

"You bring him up to shame me?"

I shrugged again.

"He was a Casanova, and he passed it on to his son. If he'd been man enough to stand up to T.G., things would've worked out different. But nobody was man enough for that."

"What I like about this case is how all of it is somebody else's fault."

"Oh, and it's mine? You can judge me when you have the facts. I had a bastard son and never had a thing to do with him. He had a bastard son of his own. I won't sell off any of my land to help them, even that little baby. Does that cover it?"

"Barely."

"You got that right. Once you start breaking up land it doesn't stop. You break off one piece and then they want you to break off another and another and pretty soon you've got nothing left. It's happened to everyone. They whittle you down. They get you to compromise and compromise and compromise until you stand for nothing. Well, I'm not going to do it and if that's hard on all the bastards in my family then so be it. They can kill people and kill off these frogs and help the land sharks and break all the laws on the books, and they'll have to settle it themselves. I'm making a sanctuary up here, a sanctuary from all the rotten things, and that's something that can't be compromised. Either it is or it isn't. My peregrine dream. It's all I have left."

"You chose not to have more."

"I chose? You think I chose this life? Well, detective, why do you think I waited so long, until I was forty, to take a lover outside this house? Why did I have to run away to do it? What could possibly be the reason old T.G. didn't want me lying down with another man? Is it coming to you now? How a man can do that with his daughter? How he can take her for his own and make her no good for anyone else? It was T.G. I was running away from, and when I came back here it was because I had him in my mind every time I lay down with Guillermo. He'd made it impossible for me to be normal with any man, impossible for me to be a mother, impossible for me to be anything but what I am, solitary. You think family means anything to me? You think I can choose it to be different?"

Pale and shaking, she got over to a decrepit hutch and tugged open a drawer and lifted out an old Colt revolver, aimed it at me. "I should kill you," she breathed. "You shouldn't walk around knowing that about me."

The gun trembled.

"People," she said.

Without a change of expression she swung the gun toward the wall and blasted two more holes in the photo of old T.G. She stowed the gun in the drawer. I couldn't get myself killed that year.

"I owe you those two old cars," she said. "The Cadillac and the Chevy with the fins. You'll have to tow them out. Call before you come. Now get out."

The sun was rising outside. Hah. Allison was wrapped in one of my old blankets, waiting in the fake Jeep for me.

"What did she say?"

"Listen." The old woman had gone out back, where she had the wounded and orphaned wild animals in cages. They howled, she howled. The howls rose through the tall trees toward the gray sky. I thought, At least the falcons have a chance, and the baby.